More Days with You

Seoul Stories Series
Book three

By Marilyn Jeulin

*In Loving Memory of Lilliam Guadalupe Alamo Estrada de Dixon
And Robert Warren Dixon
May their memory be a blessing*

Prologue

Lewis put away his cell phone and looked up when Seo-Yeon spoke. Not wanting to alarm her, he smoothed his features, knowing that he had a huge secret to keep. The problem was that Seo-Yeon could smell bullshit a few feet away from her.

After eight years together, she'd come to know him better than he knew himself.

"What's wrong?" She asked the moment their eyes met, not buying the blank expression he hoped was in his eyes.

Defeated, he took a deep breath in and then nodded. "He's requested another parole hearing," Lewis told her, not wanting to mention his father by name.

"I guess you'll have to go to Australia this time," Seo-Yeon said in a practical tone as she sat next to him on the couch and brought his arm around her shoulders. "I'll come with you."

"No, I don't want you near those people," Lewis replied, pulling her closer. "The last thing I want is to expose you to my siblings. They're all criminals."

"I'll kick their asses if they upset you," Seo-Yeon said, turning to face him, giving him that determined look he liked so much. "I swear, they mess with you, they mess with me."

"I don't think you handing them their arses will be a good thing," Lewis replied, keeping a straight face. She could chew anyone out and make them feel the need to apologize to her for insulting them. His family put people under for more minor things than feeling wronged. He'd been lucky to escape them and live to tell the tale.

"Well, I'm coming, so you can suck it up."

"Fine… what were you going to say before?"

"Oh, remember how Seo-Joon said that he needed Landry to go with him and that we had to fend for ourselves?" Seo-Yeon asked, referring to her older brother and his fiancée. Landry was also their Restaurant Manager, who'd taken a few days off. "Well, they took my parents with them and got married in Busan over the weekend. Eomma just called to tell me."

"They got married?" Lewis asked, thinking that eloping was definitely an appealing solution.

"Yes, Seo-Joon didn't want Landry to go through the stress of the wedding planning." She said, standing up and wrapping her arms around his waist. "Traitors, who's going to be my wedding planning buddy?"

Lewis's arms wrapped around her tightly as he kissed the top of her head.

"I'll be your buddy."

"Fine," Seo-Yeon said, meeting his eyes. "We could elope while we're in Australia."

"Do you want your parents to kill me?"

"Ah, yes, that would be bad." She told him and then got on her tip toes to kiss him.

"Hey, I thought you were trying to pick a china pattern from the list I gave you." He frowned as she shook her head and pulled away before taking her shirt off and chucking it at him. "Now, that's just rude." He sighed, running behind her and pulling her close to him.

Lewis crushed his lips against her before scooping her in his arms and taking her back to the bedroom.

Chapter one,

Seo-Yeon

A week later

After Seo-Joon and his bride, Landry had a few days to settle in their newlywed bliss, Seo-Yeon organized a wedding reception at the restaurant. Even though her brother had run off with his fiancée to Busan for a quick wedding, Seo-Yeon wasn't one to hold grudges. Especially when she still needed her brother to keep their mother in check while she planned her own wedding. Of course, she'd had to tell Seo-Joon about the wedding reception so he would actually agree to it. He was highly protective of Landry. Plus, he didn't want her to feel uncomfortable. It was a given that Landry didn't like people making a big fuss over her.

So, after Seo-Joon agreed, Seo-Yeon made sure to phone up all their friends and family and organize a wedding reception that would be a quiet affair. Hopefully, Landry wouldn't feel like running away or flying back to New York.

The restaurant's front door was open, and since all the lights inside were off, it was pretty dark. Seo-Yeon stood next to Lewis, glancing around the room. The guests were all hiding, making the place eerily quiet. Which was quite an accomplishment with sixty people in the room.

The elevator's bell dinged and made her look toward the front door. Soon she saw Seo-Joon and Landry slowly made their way toward them as he'd blindfolded his wife.

"This is ridiculous. You do remember I help run this place, right?" Landry asked, her hands in Seo-Joon's as he helped her step over the restaurant's threshold.

"Just work with me." He sighed, letting go of her hands once they were in the center of the main room, and stood behind her. He undid the blindfold as Seo-Yeon hit the lights, and Lewis and Simon popped the confetti canisters.

"Surprise!" They screamed in unison with the rest of the guests as Landry took a step back, but Seo-Joon held on to her.

"I told him they were going to scare you." Seo-Yeon sighed as she walked closer to them and gave Landry a quick hug. "Congrats."

"Sorry," Landry mumbled, looking at her.

"I'll forgive you, only because now we're sisters," Seo-Yeon told her sincerely as Landry nodded.

"Yes, we are." She replied as Lewis squeezed between them to give her a quick hug.

"I don't forgive you," Lewis joked with a wink as Mrs. Seok hit his arm.

"Sorry, Eomeoni," he said to his future mother-in-law, using the familiar term for mom. He bowed slightly to Mrs. Seok and then took a step back to talk to Seo-Joon.

"You should stop scaring him half to death," Seo-Yeon told her mother, but she wasn't having any of it.

"What? I treat Lewis like I treat the two of you. He's also my child. Come on, Landry, there are a few people I want you to get to know." She said, taking Landry's hand in hers to lead her away.

"I'll catch up with you in a minute," Landry promised Seo-Yeon before she walked away with Mrs. Shim.

"No worries," Seo-Yeon nodded before turning to the right to go and check on the food when she walked right into Simon. "Simon! What the heck?" She asked, reaching for a few napkins as she'd walked into him and made him spill his drink all over his shirt.

"It's okay, Noona." He replied, using the word for older sister rather than her name.

Seo-Yeon looked around and then watched him pick a few napkins. "I'm sorry," Seo-Yeon said, glancing around for Simon's wife. "Where's your Lorena?"

"She's sitting on her own." He said before clearing his throat. "Do you think you could talk to her for a bit?"

Seo-Yeon hesitated for a moment before she looked at Lorena and then sighed. "She looks pitiful."

"She doesn't feel very well, but she wanted to come and see everyone."

"Fine, I'll go talk to her," Seo-Yeon told him, then glanced toward the entrance. "Just so you know, Tae-Hyung is bringing Sarah." She explained, knowing Simon was still upset about the incident with Tae-Hyung and Lorena.

Tae-Hyung had a fling with Lorena when they were touring Mexico. Simon hadn't been there as he was filming a drama. When Lorena landed in Seoul and Tae-Hyung met her again, he'd tried to continue the fling. However, Lorena and Simon's chemistry had been so intense she'd turned Tae-Hyung down. Annoyed that Simon, the so-called priest, was dating her, Tae-Hyung then released a short clip of himself and Lorena having sex.

None of it mattered in Seo-Yeon's eyes. She was also sure that Tae-Hyung was more than sweet on Simon's twin sister, Sarah. But that girl wasn't giving him the time of day other than to be his friend. And although all of that was old history, Simon hadn't been able to let go of the humiliation he and Lorena had felt. Seo-Yeon also liked to see him get that murderous look in his eyes whenever she mentioned Tae-Hyung. It was always nice to see that Simon wasn't really that good, to be true.

Simon was trying hard not to lose his mind, but the blinking had intensified. "Wh-why?"

"Because he offered to escort her when they met each other."

"They met… where did they… why did they?"

Seo-Yeon bit her lip and then cleared her throat so she wouldn't laugh. "Shouldn't you be like… nice to him? He apologized and groveled at Lorena's feet when you guys returned to Korea."

"He's still a dick," Simon said before his ears turned pink.

"You should be careful. You don't want people to overhear you and then run with it and write a horrible expose on your band. Imagine what the fans would say."

Simon glanced quickly around them and then sighed. "Noona, just don't tell me anymore. I don't really want to think about Sarah wasting her time with Tae-Hyung."

"I don't think she's wasting her time." She said as he opened his mouth. "I think she's toying with him, giving him a bit of his own medicine." She smirked before walking toward Lorena.

Simon's wife was a glamorous Hollywood star. Seo-Yeon had met her a handful of times, but it wasn't like they were close. She always seemed to be a bit more guarded than Seo-Yeon's sister-in-law Landry, and Landry was pretty much a hard nut to crack when they first met. It could be said that for being Americans, Landry and Lorena were quite the opposite of the friendly American stereotype. Additionally, Lorena was taller than almost every other woman in the room. Seo-Yeon couldn't help but feel a bit intimidated.

"Hi, Lorena," Seo-Yeon said, putting on her biggest smile when she reached her.

"Hi, Seo-Yeon," Lorena replied confidently in Korean as she stood up to greet Seo-Yeon.

"Wow, you're so tall on those heels." Seo-Yeon blurted out in English, and Lorena rewarded her with a funny face.

"I know, but at least I'm still shorter than Simon."

"True," Seo-Yeon replied. "Can I get you something? Have you had anything to eat? Food, champagne?"

"No, alcohol." She said, clearing her throat.

"Oh?" she said absently before looking at Lorena's tiny bump and then looking back into her eyes. "Oh!"

"No one knows," she said, panicked as she looked around.

"I can keep a secret," Seo-Yeon promised as she held up her pinkie.

"Thank you," Lorena said as she linked her pinkie to Seo-Yeon's.

"Yaksok," Seo-Yeon whispered in Korean as Lorena nodded. "Come on, let's get you some food." She added, leading Lorena to the buffet area, so they could eat. A simple thought crossed her mind then. Everything was changing around them, but their friendships somehow grew and got stronger. She caught Lewis's eye for a moment and winked at him before he lifted his glass of champagne.

"Hey," Sarah greeted them, joining Lorena and Seo-Yeon at the buffet bar. "I'm sorry I'm so late, but my meeting took longer than I thought."

"It's fine. Seo-Joon and Landry have only been here for like ten minutes." Lorena told her as Sarah grabbed a plate that Seo-Yeon gave her.

"Where's Tae?" Seo-Yeon asked.

"I don't know," Sarah replied as she started piling food on her plate.

"You don't know?" Seo-Yeon repeated, and Sarah shrugged.

"If it's because of me, I can walk away," Lorena said in a half-joking manner as Sarah looked up and shook her head.

"Nah, he gave me a lift and left. He probably has a hot date or something."

"And you're not upset?" Lorena asked, frowning as Sarah grabbed the chopsticks.

"Nah, he's really not my type," Sarah replied, walking away to find a seat.

"What do you think she's up to?" Lorena asked Seo-Yeon, who shrugged.

"She's your sister-in-law. Maybe you should find out."

"I don't think so. Sarah's really prickly when you try to pry."

"Ask Simon to ask her then," Seo-Yeon nodded.

"She'll stab him," Lorena said before meeting Seo-Yeon's eyes.

"And I quite like him alive."

"I guess we'll have to wait and see," Seo-Yeon said, slightly defeated. She was sure that Sarah liked Tae-Hyung, but he'd been such an ass to Lorena that it was hard to tell if Sarah would ever fall for him.

Maybe it wasn't a bad idea. After all, Simon hadn't forgiven him yet. She shook her head to make her hair fall away from her eyes as she took the two plates and walked toward Lewis. Lewis was actually the only person who never spoke badly about Tae-Hyung. He'd actually defended him a few times. Maybe because they both share a similar background.

Seo-Yeon frowned, glancing toward Sarah, and then bit her lip as an idea formed in her mind. Maybe all Sarah and Tae-Hyung needed was a slight push. She could push them off the cliff of what if's and into a sea of romance.

Chapter two,

Lewis

Lewis winked at Seo-Yeon as she handed him the plate of food and then watched her walk away again. He sighed, slightly aggravated because all he wanted was to hug her for a few minutes.

"Hyung," Simon said, looking at Lewis.

"Yes, I'm listening."

"You're definitely not." Seo-Joon chuckled as he had some more of the food.

"I'm listening," Lewis said for a second time and focused on Simon.

"So, what will happen if your dad gets parole?"

"I don't know. At least I don't live in Australia, so he can't come after me." Lewis said, shrugging.

"Would he?" Seo-Joon asked with a frown as they huddled up closer together.

"I don't know, but he has people, and those people have people," Lewis explained before he pulled away to ensure that no one was paying attention to them. "Then there are my siblings. My brothers and sisters haven't exactly forgiven me for continuously blocking his parole hearings with my letters."

"They wouldn't— erm, come to Seoul, right?" Simon asked worriedly.

"That's why I don't want Seo-Yeon to come with me, but she's …
you know how she is."

"Yes, I doubt that she'll let you go on your own," Seo-Joon said
after a pause.

"I've tried to persuade her to stay; I'm even thinking about talking to
Eomeoni about it." He said, meaning Seo-Joon and Seo-Yeon's
mother.

"Are you insane?" Simon asked in disbelief.

"What do you suggest I do? My brothers and sisters, they're all bad
people. If Seo-Yeon comes with me to Australia, she could be in real
danger. That's why I left, and I've never been back."

"Maybe you should take a bodyguard with you," Simon said as
Lewis offered him a look of disbelief.

"No, no, Simon's right. Maybe you do need someone with you."
Seo-Joon told him. "It's not insane to think they might want you to
back down and use whatever means."

"Come on, guys, that's not… they wouldn't hurt me. It's against the
family code."

"The last time your father was up for parole, they sent you a letter
stating you were no longer part of the family," Seo-Joon said,
looking in Lewis' eyes. "You can't take this threat lightly. They're a
danger not only to you but also to my sister."

"I'll ask David if he can recommend a really bad-ass bodyguard."
Simon offered. "I mean, I think his brother or his cousin is also a
bodyguard, and he's trained just like David. He could take out a few
bad people if necessary."

"You've been watching too many movies," Lewis replied, glancing toward Seo-Yeon.

"Lewis, Hyung, just listen to us," Seo-Joon said pleadingly. "If not for your sake, for Seo-Yeon's."

After he chatted with Simon and Seo-Joon, Lewis checked on the food and the drinks, ensuring that the guests could eat and drink to their heart's content. He was about to go back to talk to Landry and Lorena, who seemed to be getting on like a house on fire, when he saw Seo-Yeon walking toward him. She took Lewis's hand and pulled him with her to the back of the restaurant, where the office was located, far from prying eyes. He frowned, following her, and then walked in the room as she let go of his hand.

"What's wrong?" he asked as Seo-Yeon locked the door behind them and made sure the small screen was pulled down over the window on the door. He arched an eyebrow as she turned around and then shook her head.

"I need sex," Seo-Yeon said, lifting her skirt.

"Are you insane? Your parents are in the restaurant?" he hissed as she shook her head and chucked her underwear at the chair near the desk.

"That's precisely why we're here. I thought the bathroom would be a bit too in their face." She said, pushing him against the chair before he sighed and then looked into her eyes.

"If you don't want to marry me, this is one sure way to do me in."

"I'm going to do you, not do you in." She murmured against his lips before kissing him deeply as she straddled him.

Lewis kissed her back, wrapping his arms around her before his hand moved up her side and cupped her breast. He groaned as she pushed his free hand between her legs and brushed his lips down her neck.

"You're so naughty sometimes." He whispered before biting her skin as he teased her.

"That's why you like me so much." She purred, pushing off his lap to undo his pants.

"I like all of you; naughtiness's just an added bonus." He said, and a moan escaped his lips when she let her lips close over him.

Lewis's hand pushed her hair away from her face as he watched her for a moment, thinking he'd really lucked out. Seo-Yeon was articulate, hardworking, sexy, and compassionate. She meant the world to him, and he had vowed to keep her safe. His eyes closed as his head rested against the back of the chair, as her lips pulled away and the heat from her body engulfed him.

His hands rested on her hips while she rocked against him. Lewis's lips crushed against hers once more. His whole body wanted to explode the faster she moved against him, and when she let out a loud moan, he moved his hand over her mouth.

A soft giggle escaped her lips, making him feel like he'd stepped under a cool waterfall on a hot summer day. He kissed her again when her body quivered in his arms.

Lewis kissed her deeply, his body feeling spent, still nestled deep inside her. His hand pushed her hair away from her neck, kissing her skin tenderly.

"You're going to be the death of me." He murmured against her skin. Seo-Yeon rewarded his effort with a smirk before kissing his forehead.

"You'll die happy." She whispered as there was a loud knock on the door. "Shit." She hissed as she looked at it, covering Lewis's mouth with her hand.

"Seo-Yeon," Landry called from outside the door.

"Well, it could have been worse… it could have been my mother." She said, pushing her skirt down and walking over to the door before she opened it.

Lewis sighed, trying to cover himself when Landry looked from Seo-Yeon to him.

"Oh, sorry, but your Eomma's looking for you," Landry nodded.

"It's fine. We were just checking something." Seo-Yeon said, glancing at Lewis with a smile.

"Uh-huh… well, make sure to wipe the lipstick off Lewis's face, or your mom will lose it," Landry said before she bit her lip to stop herself from laughing, probably, before she walked away.

"I'm dead… I'm dead." Lewis sighed, watching Seo-Yeon as she looked for her underwear.

"It'll be fine. Just wash your face." She grabbed a lipstick from her handbag hanging from the door and then applied it. She made sure her hair wasn't too messed up before giving him a lustful look.

"Later, I will turn you inside out like a sock." She added before she left the room.

Lewis stared at the door in disbelief before he finished zipping his pants again. "She's really looking forward to killing me."

Chapter three,

Seo-Yeon

Three months later

The doctor's office suddenly felt much smaller as she sat on the edge of her seat. Seo-Yeon's ears began to ring, and she knew that she had to concentrate on something other than the doctor's words. She blinked a few times, but no tears fell. What stung the most was the last words the doctor spoke. The words echoed in her mind. *Getting pregnant would require a miracle. If I were you, I wouldn't hold my breath.*

Her eyes blinked a few times, her eyes prickling badly, but no tears fell.

"But there's a chance?" Lewis asked, full of hope cutting through Seo-Yeon's heart.

"There's always a chance, but it's a minimal chance, Mr. Parker. It would be better for us to go over your choices." The doctor replied coldly.

Seo-Yeon stopped listening when the doctor started listing what they could do. In-vitro, adoption, surrogates. It didn't matter. The probability of her having a child was less than ten percent.

"I can't do this now." She stood up and then fixed her eyes on the doctor. "Thanks for your time." Her voice sounded so different, maybe because she felt her heart had been ripped out of her chest. She walked to the door and heard Lewis offering his apologies to the doctor before she slammed the door behind her.

When Lewis caught up with her, she yanked her arm away from him and glared. "Why were you apologizing? What did you do wrong?"

"Come on, Seo-Yeon, don't lash out." He said, reaching for her hand and linking their fingers together. "Don't shut me out either."

"This is a nightmare." She said and then let go of his hand again before she sat on one of the benches outside the hospital.

"If I sit down, are you going to stay put?" Lewis asked, trying to make her smile, but she gave him another death glare.

"How is it possible?" Her voice broke and the cracks spread through her whole body. She was imploding in grief for a child that she would never be able to hold in her arms, let alone carry one in her belly.

"We'll find a way. He said that we could try in-vitro or other things."

"I don't want that." She said, looking at him.

"We don't have to have kids," Lewis said, holding her hand. "Unless you want to, and we can explore all avenues."

"I don't want a child like that," Seo-Yeon said as her eyes pooled. "It feels like I would be defying God's plan."

Lewis nodded and then kissed her hand. "We can always adopt."

"And then get questions like Oh my gosh, why are you raising someone else's kid?" She asked as the tears streamed down her cheeks.

"Who cares? You want children. I want children. There are tons of children out there who need kick-ass parents." He said and then leaned closer. "We're the kick-ass parents. We can have our own band of misfits. And tights."

"What?" She asked with a strangled laugh as she looked at him and then shook her head. "You're insane sometimes." Another laugh left her body as he pulled her into his arms.

"This is not the end of the road. Maybe this is what God wants us to do. He wants us to go out there and find our children." He said and then took a deep breath in closing his eyes. "Ah, can you see them?"

"What?"

"Close your eyes." He said and then placed a hand over her eyes. "See them? They're not that far from us, just waiting, and when we all find each other, they'll be the happiest children in the world, and we'll be the luckiest parents. Screw what the rest of the society will say. They'll be our children, and we'll love them because they're ours."

"They? How many kids do you want to adopt?"

"Well, you need eleven to have a full football team."

"E—Eleven?"

"I thought if I said twenty-two as in an Australian Rules Football team, you would refuse to marry me." He smirked.

"Eleven it is then." She said, nodding as he dried the tears from her cheeks.

"We'll make it work, and you'll have that house that you want, full of kids, screaming and fighting,… and screaming." He promised before kissing her tenderly. "Loads of screaming." He said as she pulled him closer for another kiss.

"Get a room." Seo-Joon's voice said as Lewis pulled away to look at him.

"What are you doing here?" Lewis asked as he stood up and then helped Seo-Yeon up.

"Eomma wants to have lunch. Landry's with Appa seeing an old friend of Appa's."

"Is he still trying to convince her to get the new treatment?" Seo-Yeon asked.

"Yeah," he nodded. "What's wrong?" he asked as he looked at his sister.

Seo-Yeon cleared her throat and then shrugged.

"We just got some … We did a few tests to check our fertility because we've been trying for a baby for a few months, and nothing was happening." She said while Lewis brought her hand to his lips and kissed it gently. "The doctor pretty much said that we can't have a baby."

"What?" Seo-Joon frowned, pulling them both into a hug. "I'm sorry, Seo-Yeon, Lewis." He said, patting their backs gently.

"It's not the end of the world," Lewis said, shrugging. "Come on, there are loads of kids in need of parents. I'm sure when Simon finds out, he and Lorena will come up with a full list of kids they know from their various charity work, and I'll get my football team." He joked as Seo-Yeon nodded.

"Only eleven." She reminded him as Seo-Joon looked between them.

"An adoption is a great option," Seo-Joon told them as Seo-Yeon arched an eyebrow.

"Seriously? Didn't you once say that you couldn't adopt a child?" She asked, looking right into his eyes.

"Well, if I'd known how crazy things would be for me… I would have probably pushed to adopt a child. So, you two… go for it. It's going to be amazing. You two will be amazing parents." He said confidently as Seo-Yeon hugged him again.

"Thank you, Oppa," Seo-Yeon said, using the word for older brother.

"You'll be a great Mom, no matter how that baby comes to you." He said as his phone went off. "I should really hurry, or Eomma will kill me." He said, hugging Seo-Yeon again. "I'll call you later on." He nodded to Lewis and then walked toward the hospital's front door.

Lewis walked with Seo-Yeon to the car and kissed her hand before opening the door for her to climb in. She thanked him, sitting down and pulling at the seat belt for a moment, regretting not having told her brother not to say a word to their Eomma. She didn't really want to discuss this with her today.

"I feel like having something sweet," Lewis said, glancing in her direction once he was behind the wheel.

"Ice cream?"

"Let's get a big cake." He said and then looked toward the front to pull out of the parking spot. "And ice cream."

"We don't have to." Seo-Yeon knew what he was trying to do, and though it was sweet, she didn't think eating her feelings would help in this situation.

"I can get everything ready, call Lorena, Landry, and Sarah, and disappear for a while." He told her as they exited the car park.

"Let's just stay together until work starts." She said, looking at him.

"We can take off work tonight," Lewis said matter of fact as they stopped at the traffic light.

"I'd rather work."

"Fine, we'll get ice cream and cake and take it to work," Lewis said, turning on the turn signal so they could go to the ice cream shop closest to the Lotte World where their restaurant was located.

"Thank you, Darling." She said, tilting her head and looking outside the window, wondering how many other dreams wouldn't come true. It was depressing, but she couldn't think of anything else. She'd wanted to find the one and have children, a house full of them. Children running through the house, children grabbing onto her ankles, her hands giving her sloppy kisses and warm hugs. Seo-Yeon closed her eyes, tears streaming down her cheeks again. It was clear that Lewis knew that she was crying when he suddenly turned on the radio. She tried hard not to make a sound. Classical music had always been soothing, but it didn't help now. Her heart was truly broken. And as he let silence comfort her, his hand took hers and squeezed it tightly.

Chapter four

Lewis,

After closing the restaurant that night, Lewis and Seo-Yeon said goodbye as she was off to meet her friends. Once he was alone, Lewis tried to figure out how to make things easier on Seo-Yeon and whatever worries she had about their future as a family.

After texting Seo-Joon and Simon, he finished cleaning the last of the tables and walked back to the kitchen to prepare a few dishes that they could eat. He cooked a few kimchi pancakes and a seafood one, then grabbed two bottles of Makgeolli from the fridge and the bowls before walking to the restaurant's front.

Seo-Joon and Simon arrived together shortly after Lewis opened a window and lit up a cigarette. He sighed, putting it out when he saw Simon's disapproving look.

"Don't lecture me. I've had a shit day." He said, wagging his finger.

"I wouldn't, Hyung," Simon replied, following him to the table and taking his seat.

"Did you tell him?" He asked Seo-Joon when Simon looked between the two of them.

"No, I thought you would want to do that yourself," Seo-Joon said, grabbing the chopsticks.

"What's wrong?" Simon asked after the silence extended between them.

"We went to see a doctor because Seo-Yeon wanted to make sure that we can have kids. The restaurant is finally doing well enough for us not to worry about money." Lewis began as he poured the Makgeolli in the tin bowls. "We can't have children." He said after a pause and swallowed hard.

"Sorry, Hyung," Simon said, sincerely patting Lewis's arm.

"It's fine, "Lewis said dismissively. "I never really envisioned myself as a father. When I realized that Seo-Yeon was it for me, I thought it might be good to have a child who looks just like her." A smile settled on his lips before he downed the contents of the bowl and then settled it on the table. "Seo-Yeon's not taking it well." He added.

"What can we do?" Simon asked, pulling his eyebrows together.

"Well, she's got the girls with her today, and I got you guys," Lewis told them with a grin. "I just think adoption will be the best for us."

"But of course, people freak out when you mention adoption. I know my parents will, so we'll have to probably start talking about it before you guys decide on anything." Seo-Joon nodded.

"Well, if it helps, Lorena and I started the adoption process with Father Matteo's orphanage before we found out she was pregnant," Simon said without missing a beat. "We actually got approved to adopt a child and have a baby on the way."

"What?" Lewis asked, blinking as he looked at him. "And you're just saying it like that?"

"He's all kinds of grown-up," Seo-Joon said as he filled up the bowls again. "Two kids, and it's not even a year's since he got married."

"I guess if your Eomma knows that Simon and Lorena adopted, she won't be too harsh on us when we bring it up," Lewis said with a deep frown staring at the makgeolli in the bowl. "Come on, let's eat." He said, cutting up the seafood pancake, then the kimchi one. "Eomma will be happy if you guys are happy. She'll just worry about stupid people. Sometimes people don't mean it in a bad way, but they say stuff that is … foolish." Seo-Joon told Lewis, who offered him a grateful smile.

"I guess," he conceded. "I just want Seo-Yeon to be happy, and she thinks if God isn't giving us a child the normal way, then we're meant to adopt."

"I'm sure that God has a plan," Simon said enthusiastically. "And that's for you two to be the best parents. If you want to start any proceedings, we should talk to Father Matteo."

"Of course," Lewis said after popping some food in his mouth. "I'll appreciate any help in this matter. Especially since you know everyone so well at the orphanage."

"Of course."

Lewis glanced at Seo-Joon, whose eyes were on the food, but he wasn't eating. A pang of guilt shot through him before he had more of the kimchi pancake. Maybe it'd been a bit self-centered to talk about this when Landry and Seo-Joon couldn't have children either, and she was not doing that well.

"You should try Australia as well," Seo-Joon said after a pause. "I mean here and Australia. It might be best to try several places."

"Yes, I guess." Lewis offered him a half-smile which Seo-Joon returned.

"You and Seo-Yeon will be amazing parents." He added before he had more of the makgeolli.

"How's Landry doing?" Lewis asked as Seo-Joon shrugged.

"It's early days, but she's doing good mentally."

"I'm taking her to the movies with me tomorrow night," Simon said with a smirk as Seo-Joon hit his shoulder.

"Stop being all cute to my wife. Be all cute to your wife."

"Hey, I can't help it if Noona thought she was dating below her when she met me." He joked.

"This brat." He said, hitting Simon's shoulder playfully but with enough strength making Simon complain.

"That really hurt, Hyung." Simon sighed as he patted his own shoulder.

"You shouldn't hit him. He got a new tattoo right there on the shoulder." Lewis said matter of fact before he got up to prepare the kimchi egg fried rice.

"You got a tattoo?" Seo-Joon asked, pulling at Simon's t-shirt.

"Hyung, stop. Stop!" Simon whined as he shook his head and then pulled at his shirt.

"You don't have to show me your abs." Seo-Joon teased him as Simon let out an exasperated sigh.

"It hurts so much." He said before he showed him the small tattoo on his shoulder.

"That's… that's really tiny. Hey Lewis, do you have a magnifying glass out there?" He called jokingly as he stood up to have a better look.

"Very funny," Simon replied with a roll of his eyes. "It's a lot bigger than the artist said it would be."

Lewis returned with a small torch and then turned it on. He then shone the bright light on Simon's shoulder. "Use this."

"Oh, there, now, I can see it."

"It's not that small," Simon grumbled again.

"Wow, Simon's got a tattoo." Seo-Joon sighed. "The fangirls are going to go crazy."

"Hope they don't find out. His Eomma will kill him and Lorena." Lewis said as he walked back to the kitchen to get the rice.

"Why Temperance? I mean, the meaning suits you."

"That's Lorena's real name," Simon said with a huge smile.

"Really? Wow, it suits her too." Seo-Joon said as Lewis placed the dish with the rice on the table.

"So, what's the other flower?" Seo-Joon asked, sitting beside him. "The Mugunghwa I know very well, but that other flower?"

"It's an orange blossom," Simon explained. "I wanted both to represent us, me and Lorena. Even though Lorena doesn't like people calling her Temperance, it is her name."

"And Haru Haru?" Seo-Joon asked, arching an eyebrow.

"A promise to take everything day by day," Simon explained. "Also, we'll name her Haru if it's a girl."

"Aw, that's adorable," Lewis said before having a spoonful of the rice.

"It is indeed," Seo-Joon said, patting his back, careful not to hit his shoulder again, while Simon pulled down the shirt.

"I'm glad you like it since you'll be the godfathers." He said, looking at them.

"Of course, Seo-Joon and I will be the best godparents ever. No boy will ever be able to steal her away from you. And if it's a boy, we'll teach him how to prank you forever." Lewis grinned as he lifted his bowl of makgeolli.

"Hear, hear," Seo-Joon said, bumping his bowl against Lewis.

He'd lost count of the number of times he'd been grateful to have Simon and Seo-Joon in his life. Tonight, no matter how many times he'd said the same prayer, he would pray for their lives to be filled with love, laughter, and health. They were indeed his brothers, and he knew things would get tough for him and Seo-Yeon in the future; however, he had them, and that thought would comfort him all his life.

Chapter five

Seo-Yeon

The restaurant was packed, but the girls had managed to snatch a table far away from most of the noisy company dinners. Once the food arrived at the table, Seo-Yeon felt her stomach growl. She'd not eaten a lot during the last few days. Being surrounded by everyone suddenly helped her feel relaxed. Seo-Yeon knew then that she could let her repressed feelings out.

"Is Sarah coming?" Landry asked, glancing to the door.

"She went back to London last night," Lorena explained.

"Did she call after arriving back home?" Seo-Yeon asked Lorena as everyone started digging in.

"No. Simon left her a message last night, and I tried texting this morning, but she seemed busy."

"That guy she's dating is so handsome," Landry said before taking a sip of her water. "He's so tall as well. I think Seo-Joon said he's taller than Simon."

"Apparently," Lorena said, nodding. "I just don't know. He seems a bit… too good to be true."

"Ah, so like Simon?" Seo-Yeon teased her.

"Sorta." Lorena nodded. "I don't know. When we met them in London, it was a bit weird."

"Weird how?" Landry asked curiously.

"Simon thinks I'm reading too much into it."

"Go on," Seo-Yeon prompted her.

"He doesn't like her talking to her friends when they're together."

"Well, she should pay attention to him." Landry chimed in.

"I know, but it's just how he talks to her about it. Even us being there made me feel uncomfortable."

"Or maybe the pregnancy has made you paranoid," Seo-Yeon told her, thinking Sarah would know not to get into a controlling or destructive relationship. She'd always been advised by her brother, and she'd always listened to Simon.

"So, what did you want to talk about?" Landry asked before taking a small portion of the chicken on her plate.

"The bloodwork and all the test results came back a few days ago," Seo-Yeon announced as she kept her eyes on the food.

"And?" Lorena asked, putting down the piece of chicken that she'd just bitten into.

"It wasn't good news."

"I'm sorry to hear that, Seo-Yeon," Landry said, and Seo-Yeon nodded before meeting their eyes.

Feeling utterly broken once more, the tears spilled without her even noticing.

"Ah, this is so stupid, we can adopt," Seo-Yeon said, reaching for a tissue in her purse.

"Of course, but it's good to let it out." Landry frowned as she kept her eyes on Seo-Yeon.

"Simon knows all the people at the orphanage. I mean the ones who help the kids get fostered or adopted." Lorena said, patting Seo-Yeon's back.

"Lewis said that." A smile pulled at her lips, though she still somehow felt like she'd failed.

"But if you still feel like letting it all out, we're here for you," Landry said before taking a bite of the chicken.

"Thank you, I'm grateful… really grateful that I can talk to you two like this." She said, meaning it. She'd gotten closer to Lorena in the last couple of months, and even more so to Landry.

"Of course, we're family," Lorena told her, and Seo-Yeon couldn't help but smile.

"We are family, that's true," Seo-Yeon affirmed and then shook her head as she tried to keep the tears under control. "But I don't want this to be all about me," Seo-Yeon added and smiled at Lorena. "How are you feeling?"

"I'm okay, my back's beginning to hurt sometimes in the afternoon, especially if I've been on my feet for a bit, but it's not too bad," Lorena explained.

"Will you take time off work then? I know Simon wanted you to, but it seems that you enjoy doing the variety shows as much as the Korean hosts like having you over." Seo-Yeon bit her lip, watching her.

"Not yet; I'm having too much fun, even when I inadvertently insult people with my bad Korean," Lorena said, a giggle escaping her lips.

"What about you?" Seo-Yeon asked Landry. "How are you really feeling?"

"I'm okay, I'm just, well— for now, I'm good." Landry nodded.

"Do you know when the chemo will end?"

"Soon. I already have a ton of medical journals to read with Seo-Joon as your dad found another cancer expert who will fly to Korea." She shrugged slightly.

Seo-Yeon felt terrible about having brought up her problems when Landry and Seo-Joon's were so much bigger than hers. Their problem was to keep Landry alive. So, what if she couldn't carry a child, she could still find her child in the orphanage, and she would love them just as much. She had to stop feeling sorry for herself.

Seo-Yeon joined Landry and Lorena outside the restaurant after paying for the meal. She frowned, noticing Lorena and Landry huddling up, a look of distress on Lorena's face.

"What's wrong?"

"I have two missed calls from Sarah, but she's not picking up now," Lorena replied as Seo-Yeon grabbed her own phone from her bag and dialed Sarah's number.

"I'll get the cab," Landry said as Lorena took her hand in hers.

"No, I'll do it, hold on. Maybe she'll reply to Seo-Yeon." Lorena said, letting go of Landry's hand, and walked to the sidewalk's edge.

"She still feels like Sarah doesn't like her," Landry muttered so only Seo-Yeon could hear her.

"She likes her fine, but I think she's still embarrassed over the Tae-Hyung thing," Seo-Yeon whispered.

"Well, that wasn't her fault. Sarah dealt with the whole thing, and he apologized. I think she's too hard on herself. Lorena really wants a close relationship with her."

"She'll just have to learn to wait," Seo-Yeon said as the call was sent to voice mail. "She's not answering now."

"Well, at least she has us for now," Landry said absently as Seo-Yeon arched an eyebrow.

"Are you planning on going somewhere/"

"No," Landry laughed softly and then shrugged. "I mean until she and Sarah can be close."

"Well, it's a shame, but not everyone can have such a good strong bond between sisters-in-law, like you and me."

"True." Landry agreed as Lorena waved at them.

"Ah, finally, let's go," Seo-Yeon said, linking arms with Landry and walking toward the cab.

The cab driver wasn't amused when they told him that he would have to drive to Guri and back, but he seemed a lot friendlier once he recognized Lorena. Once they dropped Landry off with Seo-Joon, the driver took them back to Cheongdam-dong, where Simon and Lorena bought an apartment after getting married.

Lorena answered the phone call on the first ring and then sighed, relieved when Sarah spoke.

"I'm sorry, Unnie, I was going to call you back, but I have terrible allergies today. I don't know why. It's probably all the pollen." She said after Lorena put her on speakerphone.

"It's fine, Seo-Yeon, and I tried calling you because I couldn't answer the call before. I think it'd dropped or something." Lorena replied, looking at Seo-Yeon. "Are you okay? Do you need us to send you anything?" She asked, putting Sarah on speakerphone.

"I'm fine, you know I can find everything I need in London. This is your old city. You should know that." Sarah replied, but her voice didn't sound as cheerful as usual.

"Is that model giving you a hard time?" Seo-Yeon asked bluntly.

"No, no, it's just allergies."

"Fine. Just let us know if you need us." Seo-Yeon said in a stern tone.

"Of course, is Landry Unnie with you too?"

"No, we dropped her off first. We're almost at Lorena's house now."

"Ah, when I go back to Seoul, we should all go out to the noraebang and eat chimaek. I want to have a girl's night out." Sarah said, knowing the girls all loved chicken and beer. There was a commotion, and Seo-Yeon heard a door opening and closing on Sarah's end. "I must go. The cat just pushed a few things to the floor." She said hurriedly as Seo-Yeon frowned.

"Sure, call us back whenever."

"Yes, bye."

Lorena's expression was one of worry as Seo-Yeon cleared her throat. "She's fine."

"I hope so," Lorena said, then looked out the window when the taxi pulled over outside her building.

"When's your bodyguard coming back from his honeymoon?" She asked, arching an eyebrow noticing Simon staggering toward the cab.

"Ten more days. Simon already hired two more bodyguards." She said, glancing at him. "He drinks so much whenever he meets up with Seo-Joon and Lewis." She said, amused.

"They're terrible, and then they get so clingy. *Hyung, I love you. Do you know how much I love you, Hyung?*" Seo-Yeon said before pretending to ugly cry.

"Shush, he's going to hear you. See you later. Thanks for tonight." Lorena told her and then climbed out of the cab into Simon's arms. Seo-Yeon grinned at them and waved goodbye once the taxi pulled away from the parking spot. Her eyes remained on the buildings. They weaved in and out of traffic. The weight that had been on her shoulders was finally gone.

Chapter six

Lewis

It was pouring as Lewis arrived at the post office to pick up the mail for the restaurant from the PO box that they'd set up. After gathering their correspondence, he noticed a familiar envelope and moved to the counter to take a better look. The mail was placed neatly on the counter, while his eyes fixed on the envelope, Lewis swallowed hard. He looked around and then ripped the envelope open, skimming through the letter. The word parole jumped at him like a knife cutting through his body before he reached the last line of the letter. We hope you'll submit your statement before the end of the following month if you have any objections.

Lewis ran a hand through his hair and closed his eyes, gripping the letter tightly in his right hand. He'd hoped since he'd not heard anything else from Michael, his friend and lawyer in Australia, that his father had desisted from the idea of getting parole once again. Still, it seemed that he and his lawyer were just buying time.

After picking everything up, Lewis walked out of the post office to his car, settling the mail in the vehicle's back seat before getting behind the steering wheel. He took a deep breath in, but the anger was burning hot in the pit of his stomach as he hit the steering wheel several times thinking about his father. He really had a high opinion of himself, was the first thing Lewis thought.

Anger turned into guilt as Lewis revved up the engine. If he'd stayed behind, his mother would still be alive. He would have ensured that she was safe and living in Korea with him. She would be living in a new country, but most importantly, she would be alive. He rolled to a stop at the traffic light. A memory of his mother singing in the rain filtered through his thoughts, melting the guilt away and giving space to only grief.

He turned right and then left, not losing his composure before taking the highway. Lewis needed to drive to the fish market then go straight to the restaurant, but the pain made it hard for him to even concentrate on the to-do list that he had in his mind. Maybe his older brother, Theo, was right. Lewis was responsible, just like his father, for their mother's death. She wouldn't have ever been abused if he'd stayed to be their father's punching bag. His father would have never killed her.

Once back at the restaurant, Lewis walked into the office and smiled at Seo-Yeon. She was surrounded by hundreds of folders on the desk. He sighed, wondering how she could get anything done. His desk was extremely tidy, and there were no papers on it because he kept everything filed. Still, Seo-Yeon knew where everything was in the mess she'd created, and sometimes he misplaced his stapler only to have to ask her for hers. So maybe she had figured out something that he hadn't about tidying up.

"Are you okay?"

"Yeah, I got all the stuff from the P.O." He glanced at the small pile of boxes and letters as she stood up and walked around her desk.

"Ah, I guess these are the new coffee samplers." She said before she grabbed the box knife from the desk.

"Yes, be careful with that."

"Don't worry," Seo-Yeon told him as she deftly opened the box. "What are those?"

"The rest is just bills and a letter from Australia."

"So, he formally asked for the parole hearing again?" Seo-Yeon asked as Lewis nodded.

"I don't know why he can't stay put. He only has two more years in jail. That's such a small amount of time." He ran his hands through his hair. "I mean, he could have at least tried to serve the whole sentence for the life that he took away."

"Of course." Seo-Yeon frowned, placing the box down. She walked toward him and wrapped her arms around his neck. "It's going to be fine. Even if he gets parole, he can't hurt you."

"I'm not worried about that." He sighed, pulling her onto his lap. "I'm worried about him not paying for his sins… he killed my mother, and he only got twenty-five years on appeal because of a technicality."

"Your Eomma would be so proud of the man you've become, Lewis," Seo-Yeon said soothingly, looking right in his eyes. "You have dealt with so much, but you never lost your way. You managed to turn your life around and do great things. I'm sure she's very proud of you."

"I know," he acknowledged, but he still felt grief, anger, and more than anything, guilt. The three emotions were slowly suffocating him.

Her phone pinged loudly with a message as she held on tight to Lewis. "Do you want to go to Australia and do this in person?"

"No, there's no need, really. I just need to send another letter like every other time before." He replied as he glanced at her phone as it pinged again.

"Well, what about we go there and see your mom?"

"My mom?" he asked, frowning as he met her eyes, knowing she meant a visit to the cemetery, and then glanced at the phone. "I don't know."

"I would love to meet her," Seo-Yeon said as she cupped his cheeks in her hands. "We can even get married there."

"In Australia? Are your parents coming to this imaginary wedding? Because I don't want to be killed before we go on our imaginary honeymoon." He told her. "Who's texting you?"

Seo-Yeon rolled her eyes and grabbed the phone. "Oh, Sarah was asking if I knew good secretaries since she has to hire many people once she moves back here." She explained. "That's really awesome."

"I bet she's wishing she'd stayed in the job she had before getting hired by Gracie," Lewis smirked.

"Yes, but she didn't like it, so she applied to Graciela Marquez's company. She will be a CEO and have a lot more responsibility."

"Graciela Marquez." The name rolled off his tongue as he wondered if Gracie had been indiscreet and told Sara any stories about her time dating Lewis.

"What are you thinking about?" Seo-Yeon's voice was colored by jealousy as Lewis met her eyes.

"Nothing," Lewis said, knowing he was winding her up.

"This is why I made you wait so long for me to say yes to you. You were such a manwhore." She replied, wagging her finger before walking out of the office

"Are you upset?" Lewis asked with a smirk as he followed her out of the office.

"No," she said way too fast.

"You're totally jealous, geez. That was years before I even met you."

"I'm not jealous."

"Oh, come on." Lewis wrapped his arms around her waist and kissed her neck. "No one compares to you. Plus, I think she's married as well."

"Oh, she is, to the hottest playwright in London," Seo-Yeon said, wiggling herself out of his arms.

"See, and I'm going to be married to the hottest girl in the world very soon unless she gets me killed with this elopement talk." He sighed dramatically as she turned to look at him.

"So, we're going to Australia?"

"I don't know, Seo-Yeon."

"Come on, you've not visited your mom in years, and we could invite everyone— they might come with us." She said, pouting.

"Including your parents?"

"Destination weddings are all the rage now. They'll never shut up about it and bore their friends to death." She nodded.

Lewis hesitated, staring at her before he groaned. "Fine."

"Thank you! Thank you!" She said, kissing him deeply.

Chapter seven

Seo-Yeon

Lorena fussed over the table as Seo-Yeon helped Landry walk to it. A slight disapproving shake from Seo-Yeon's head made Lorena standstill. Seo-Yeon felt her cheeks turning bright pink as she waved her hand dismissively.

"I'm sorry, I didn't mean to be rude," Seo-Yeon said, looking at Lorena. "You've outdone yourself, and I know you should be resting." She said, trying for her tone to be warmer. Sometimes, she knew it was hard to understand her because she felt like she had a firm tone of voice.

"No, you weren't," Lorena said, offering her a half-smile. "I just, well, I'm excited about hosting you tonight. It's actually the first-time you girls have come over without Simon taking over and feeding everyone." She explained as Landry looked around the table. "These are all things that I like about Miami… Mostly Cuban food, of course." She added when Seo-Yeon sat down, and then she took her seat.

"It all smells delicious," Seo-Yeon said, hoping that Landry had some appetite. The last chemo treatments were harder on her than it was the last time.

"I can't believe you cooked all of this on your own," Landry said with a slight nod. "It looks amazing."

"I'm a Miami girl at heart," Lorena replied as she waved her hands for them to serve themselves. "I might not be Cuban, but my sort of surrogate mom was. Once a month, she would buy us food from one of the restaurants in Calle Ocho, and then when the restaurant owners found out, some of them would donate the food for us." She said with a smile as her eyes clouded with tears.

"You must miss Miami a lot," Seo-Yeon said in a concerned tone as Lorena nodded.

"Seoul is really spectacular. Simon and I have been sneaking into Namsan tower late at night. It's my favorite place in the city. So, we usually go right before they close and stay for a few minutes."

"That's really cool," Landry said, eating a bit of the pork and rice with the black beans. "Oh, Lorena, this is really delicious."

"Thank you, I'm so glad you like it. There's also the Caldo de Pollo. It's chicken soup. The nuns always swore that it had restorative powers; it'll help you through it."

"I will have some, thank you." Landry nodded before having a bit of it.

"Have you been able to talk to the people building the— what is it again? Halfway house?" Seo-Yeon asked Lorena before she got some of the freshly baked bread. "I see you're putting the oven you made Simon buy to good use. The bread is so crunchy."

"Thank you." Lorena nodded. "Yes, I had a zoom meeting this morning, so I have the proposal. Since your parents were both interested in investing, I'll be meeting with them later this week."

"Is this for the homeless teens?" Landry asked.

"Yes, well, I want to make sure the kids turning eighteen and leaving the care facilities and orphanages have somewhere safe to go. The statistics are so grim. Caly and I know that well enough." She said, referring to her best friend and personal make-up artist.

"Where is Caly?" Landry asked.

"She and Min-Young had tickets to go see a musical. They said they're buying us dinner next week." She added.

"Oh, I hope it is from that fancy seafood place." Seo-Yeon joked as she had more of the food. "Bring Lewis and me a project proposal to see if we can help out." She said with a slight nod. "I mean, I would like to help out. I just don't know much about care facilities or orphanages." Her voice broke slightly. Seo-Yeon made sure not to make eye contact with them.

"It's okay," Landry said, placing her hand on Seo-Yeon's hand and then offering her a smile which Seo-Yeon mirrored. "We're all here for you."

"I know… it's just. I don't know. There's so much to process." Seo-Yeon said before dabbing her eyes with the napkin. "But first, since Lewis hasn't been back to Australia in years, I thought it would be good to have our wedding there."

"Destination wedding?" Lorena asked, surprised as she tucked into the food.

"Well, I understand if you guys don't want to travel, but I think he needs to go back and deal with the ghosts of his past."

"I don't know about Lorena and Simon, but I'm sure Seo-Joon and I can come."

"Us too, I mean unless it's after I hit seven months. The doctors said that I can't travel past seven months." Lorena explained.

"Lewis is also writing to the parole board about his dad. He's tried to get them to review his case and make him serve the last two years, rather than releasing him early."

"What? But he caused Lewis's mom's death." Landry said in an angry tone as she turned to face Seo-Yeon.

"Lewis is distraught. He's trying to hide it, but I don't want him to implode, so I think the trip will be good. He can surf and do all these things that he's not done in years, and even if we're near his family, we'll still not be that close by, and he can visit his mom's grave."

"I can only imagine. His father killed someone. He shouldn't get to leave jail before the time is served."

"Exactly," Seo-Yeon said before she smiled at Lorena. "He beat up Lewis for years. That's why he ran away when he was just thirteen." Seo-Yeon explained to her. "He never hit any of the other kids. Lewis was the youngest, and after he left, his father simply shifted his attention to Lewis's mom. He beat her up so badly that she wound up in the ICU and passed away a few days later of her injuries."

"That's horrible, poor Lewis," Lorena said, surprised as she covered her mouth with her hand.

"He's always felt guilty because he believes his mother wouldn't have been abused if he'd not run away."

"It's not his fault. He was a baby himself."

"Yes, and he was homeless for years until he managed to get on a ship and then landed in Korea, no money, no real knowledge of the language. He's lucky that he found a good sponsor who helped him get all his paperwork in order, so he could stay." She said, nodding before having more of the food. "Of course, the price he paid was to be far from his siblings, but I do believe he did the right thing," Seo-Yeon explained. "They're not good people. All of them are linked to crimes and mafia-style stuff."

"Is this why they were talking about a bodyguard?" Lorena asked Seo-Yeon, who nodded.

"Simon thinks he should hire one if he ever goes back to Australia, and I tend to agree," Seo-Yeon told her.

"It must be so sad to know you have siblings out there who are such idiots," Landry said as she had more of the soup.

"Well, we're all here for him," Lorena said as she looked at Seo-Yeon. "You guys are like family to Simon, and I want to be like a sister to you two as well."

"You are, Lorena." Seo-Yeon grinned at her before she took her hand and squeezed it gently. "I'm glad Simon and Seo-Joon found the two of you and that we all get along just fine. Like a family."

"Excellent, so if we're going to go to Australia, we should start looking up places," Landry said with a wink. "Your Eomma will be furious if she has to do the heavy lifting."

"Oh, I'm sure she'll tell everyone that I slacked— and totally love it." She said with a small laugh as the girls joined.

Chapter eight

Lewis

It'd taken about a week, but Lorena and Simon managed to present her project to prospective investors. She wanted to build a new sort of halfway house for teenagers that needed to find a job and a place to live. Lorena hoped that the housing offered a better chance for girls and boys to grow out of the care system. Lewis was thankful that Seo-Yeon wanted to get involved. Still, the fact that she wasn't talking much about her feelings, and had shut down trying IVF or a surrogate, had him slightly freaked out. He didn't want her to suffer on her own. After all, he also had problems. The doctor said it would have probably been easier to have a child together if one hadn't had problems. But since they both had issues, the possibility was one in a million.

"What's he doing here?" Landry asked in a whisper as she moved closer to Lewis, and he followed her eyes. "Is he also investing?" Lewis noticed Tae-Hyung walking into the room with his manager.

"I guess." He said and then knocked his shoulder gently with Landry's. "Are you going to hate on him forever?"

"He's a selfish jerk. And I think I can hate him forever."

"He's not that bad," Lewis said to Landry and then looked around to ensure that no one could hear them. "He's had a very rough time too." He said, looking at her. "He could be the third musketeer." He said, pointing at her and him and then Tae-Hyung.

"Well, the fans have forgiven him now. All will be forgotten in a few years, and he'll rejoin the band." Landry said, looking at him, and then shook her head.

"Try not to hate him," Lewis said as she rolled her eyes.

"Fine."

"Growing up, he had a rough time. Yes, what he did to Lorena and Simon was pretty shitty, but Tae-Hyung had a very rough time with his family. His father was an asshole just like mine, and when he died of a heart condition, Tae-Hyung's mother kicked him out of the house because she blamed him for angering the father so much he died. Sounds familiar?"

Landry's eyes welled up while following Tae-Hyung around the room. "His mother made him homeless?" She asked, and Lewis nodded his head.

"Unlike me, he chooses bravado and being a humongous knob to people when he feels inferior to them," Lewis added pensively. "He just needs someone to knock him down a peg or two and then help him again."

"Sounds like he needs therapy."

"He's actually seeing someone after Sarah suggested it."

"Well, now I feel like a total bitch." She sighed, feeling remorseful.

"We've all earned our stripes, haven't we?" He asked as she arched an eyebrow. "You, Lorena, me— Tae-Hyung."

"I guess we have." Landry nodded, her eyes returning to Tae-Hyung.

"But sometimes you can't wait for people to help you out. You must work on yourself. You have to do that yourself."

"True, but for that, you need strength. You and Lorena are the strongest people I know, and Seo-Yeon. Even though your backgrounds are so different, the three of you are determined to make a better life for yourselves. But not everyone is like that." He explained.

"I guess," Landry said as Seo-Joon walked toward them.

"Are you trying to run away with my wife? Before marrying my sister?" Seo-Joon joked, wrapping an arm around Landry's waist.

"Stop saying that. Do you want your sister to kill me?" he asked, looking around for Seo-Yeon.

"Relax, she's with Simon helping him go over the last bits of the speech."

"Good, because I don't want to die before we get married." He watched Lorena and Simon walk to the small area where the podium was.

"We should go and sit down," Seo-Joon said, patting Lewis back before leading Landry away.

Lewis took a seat next to his future parents-in-law. He looked over the folder that had been on his chair. He read the small booklet that detailed Lorena's venture. More importantly, he could see how it would help teenagers navigate their newly found independence. Lorena and Simon worked with the orphanages in Seoul and Miami. They'd also opened a halfway home to do a trial version of the services the young adults would need in Seoul. Lorena and Simon's ambitious program wanted to create as many safe places as possible for those children aging out of the care system and orphanages.

"Sorry," Seo-Yeon said to her mother, then took Lewis's hand. "They're so nervous. You wouldn't even think they're both entertainers and used to talking to people."

"Well, it's different." Seo-Yeon's mother said before she glanced at them. "It's real life. Simon has always done missionary work or helped orphans… this is his chance, and so is Lorena's to educate loads of people who don't want to help orphanages."

"At least the investors care. However, it will be hard to make things like this acceptable to many Koreans," Seo-Yeon said as her mother turned completely to face her.

"What do you mean?"

"People here don't talk about adoption … they just sweep things under the rug and ignore those children in need."

"Not all people. Just some." Her mother said before she sighed, looking as Lorena and Simon walked on the stage. "A child is a blessing no matter how it comes into the family. Look at your brother and Landry." She said, nodding toward them, sitting closer to the stage. "It's too bad they can't adopt."

"You wouldn't mind?" Seo-Yeon asked, and Lewis turned his full attention to them.

"A child is a gift from heaven. It's even a greater gift when you get to pick your child. Imagine being able to tell your child that you picked them."

Seo-Yeon let go of Lewis's hand and hugged her mother tightly.

"What? What are you doing? You're going to ruin my hair."

"Thank you, Eomma." She whispered as Lewis patted her back.

Seo-Yeon sniffled quietly after handing her a tissue and looked at him, giving him a huge smile before letting go of her mother.

"I love you." He mouthed as she nodded, leaning her head against his as they turned their attention to the presentation.

Chapter nine
Seo-Yeon

After the presentation, Seo-Yeon and Lewis walked around the different tables Simon and Lorena had set up for some of the Miami and Korean representatives. Lewis seemed a bit distracted, and she was sure that it had something to do with his friend's call. He didn't want to worry her and took the call in the back office. However, Seo-Yeon had overheard part of the chat anyway. She didn't mean to eavesdrop when she'd gone to file some of the paperwork after the CPA gave her back the books. It'd just happened.

"How much do you think we can invest?" Lewis asked as he pulled at his tie.

"I don't know. They have different tiers. We might as well not be too cheap, but not too extravagant either. Especially with the wedding and the future adoption." She said, beaming.

"Ah, I like that." Lewis turned completely to face her before brushing his lips against hers.

Seo-Yeon kissed him passionately before she felt a smack on her upper right arm.

"Eomma!" Seo-Yeon gasped, rubbing the red spot on her arm while her mother shrugged.

"You're not in private." Her mother said, walking toward Seo-Joon and Landry.

"You still can run away." Dr. Shim, Seo-Yeon's father, said to Lewis with a smirk.

"I'm good, sir," Lewis replied, looking at him, taking Seo-Yeon's hand in his.

"Sorry," Seo-Yeon sighed, mortified as her mother's eyes were on them. "I swear, if it were Seo-Joon making out with Landry, she wouldn't even bat her eyes." She muttered as Lewis pulled her to the table closest to them.

"Let's just split the money equally between the two places," Lewis said, and she understood he didn't want her to dwell on things they couldn't change. Her mother was a stickler for manners and totally against public PDA.

"Sure," Seo-Yeon said as she watched him fill out the form. "That much?"

"It's not that much," Lewis said, looking at her. "But we can make a smaller contribution if you want."

"Nah, that's good." She nodded and then looked around for her brother and Landry. "So, what did Michael want?"

"Oh, you know, he wants me to write the letter as soon as possible so he can hand it to the team that is reviewing the parole request."

"Did he say anything about your siblings?"

"Caleb got arrested, but I don't know why."

"Is that your oldest brother?"

"Yes, he's the one who took over the family business after my dad was jailed." He said, turning the page over.

"If we go to Australia, you won't have to deal with them," Seo-Yeon said, looking at him.

"Well, I don't think we'll be making any detours to Adelaide. We'll stay mainly in Sydney and see my mom there."

"Of course," Seo-Yeon said, pushing her hair behind her ear. "They don't have people in Sydney, right?"

"No, not that I know of, and Michael said they don't ever go to Sydney." Lewis turned to face her. "I know that my attitude might have scared you, but we'll hire those bodyguards Simon recommended, and we'll make sure that we're all safe."

"You really made it sound like your family runs the mafia there," Seo-Yeon said before watching him as he started writing on the forms again. "Lewis," she whispered when he didn't reply. Seo-Yeon leaned in closer to his ear and then hissed. "Are they the mafia?"

"It's sorta that way." He said and then placed the pen down before looking at her. "But I promise that nothing bad will happen."

"I really don't know if you're being serious or not."

"Seo-Yeon," he sighed, taking her hands in his. "There's a reason I don't provide that much information on them. I told you they're not good people."

"Maybe we should overthink going to Australia then."

"If that's what you want, we don't have to go. We can marry here. And Michael, he goes to the cemetery for me and lays wreaths for my mother during all the important dates." He said, tucking her hair behind her ear. "It's not a big deal. I know my mother is not there, it's just a place— with her name, but she's not there."

"I need to think about this."

"Seo-Yeon, I didn't bring up Australia. You did." He told her, holding her gaze. "I don't have any interest in going there at all. We can just go to Jeju and marry there."

"I was just trying to do something nice for you." She muttered before he kissed her cheek.

"Well, if it's that, we can leave now." He smirked as she hit his shoulder. "What? Everyone is here; we might as well just go."

"Just finish writing the information down so we can give them the money."

"Aye, aye, Captain." He teased her turning his attention to the paperwork again.

***

Later that night, Seo-Yeon poured a glass of water over two ice cubes and moved near the big windows in the living room before opening one. She fixed her eyes on the city lights before walking to the desk closest to the windows turning the computer on. She took a sip of water and settled the glass on the coaster, waiting for the browser to open. Then she started researching adoption agency sites in Korea. Her mind was full of questions, but mostly she wanted to make sure that she could bond with the baby. It was the thing that had come up the most in the parents' forum that she'd joined. Most of the parents-to-be didn't feel like they could bond with someone else's child. And she didn't want to be like that. She wanted to make sure that whoever they brought home, she would love them as much as if it was a baby from her very own belly.

"Why are you up?" Lewis asked, scratching his stomach as he walked toward the couch close to the desk.

"I can't sleep." She replied, exiting out of the browser and looking at him.

"Don't worry about my family."

"I'm not. You said I shouldn't, so I won't."

"I mean, I've been here all these years, and they've not come to see me or called or anything." He shrugged and then scratched the stubble on his face.

"Okay," Seo-Yeon replied, reaching for the glass of water.

"So, what were you doing?"

"I was just looking through parents' forums and seeing everyone's opinions on adoption."

"And?"

"There's a lot of work to do… it seems." She said with a rueful smile.

"Your mom seems to be okay with it."

"Yes, but I don't know if my dad shares those ideas."

"I'm sure he does," Lewis replied.

"We have time."

"Of course, I mean we have to get married first." Lewis reminded her with a smile as he stood up and then walked closer to her, offering his hand for her to take.

"What if I don't bond with the baby?"

"Then we will have to try really hard at being good parents."

"A baby knows when it's being rejected. That's what some of the parents said."

"Seo-Yeon, I've never met anyone you didn't love totally. Your brother, your parents, your friends. You've even adopted the wives and extended family of friends." He said, looking at her. "Our baby is out there, and we'll be great parents, but you will be the most amazing mother."

"I really hope you're right."

"I'm sure I am." He said, kissing her tenderly. "Come on, let's go back to bed."

Chapter ten

Lewis

After meeting up with some of the old military buddies, Lewis stopped to get a few things from the supermarket. He wanted to make a nice dinner for Seo-Yeon. They'd taken the night off to see how the new manager ran the restaurant with the chefs, without Lewis or Seo-Yeon breathing down their necks. Seo-Yeon had hesitated, but Landry had, in the end, convinced her that it was a good idea since she was going to take days off anyway for the honeymoon.

He placed the bags on the back of the car and then frowned as he noticed the same black van parked at the restaurant's parking near his car when he'd said goodbye to his friends. Lewis walked around and got behind the wheel, his eyes on the rearview mirror. He couldn't see anyone in the driver's seat, so he pulled out of his parking spot and then drove out of the lot, taking the first right, ensuring that he took the long way back to the apartment.

Lewis noticed the van was hot on its tail as soon as he hit the main road. He pressed the button for the phone on the steering wheel and then dialed the number of his old friend Sung-Rok who worked at the nearby precinct.

"You only call me when there's something wrong. I'm going to start believing the rumors that you don't love me anymore." Sung-Rok joked as Lewis changed lanes.

"Someone's tailing me."

"See, so direct. Where are you?"

"I'm not far from the precinct."

"Come on over then. I'll wait outside to see if I can see the car. Can I have a description?" he asked.

"Some sort of black van, but I can't see the make or model."

"Don't speed or come into the parking lot. Just drive by the precinct, and I'll note the license plate."

"Do you think my brothers would be able to do this?" Lewis asked, slightly panicked as the van was still pursuing him.

"If it's them, we'll find out. And if it's that stupid guy trying to get you and Seo-Yeon to sell to him, we'll stop him. Either way, I'll make sure to get the license plate number."

"Thanks, Hyung." He said as he took a sharp turn into a narrow street that was behind the precinct. "I'm almost there."

"Okay, I'm outside now," Sung-Rok replied.

"Turning into your street now," Lewis said as he glanced at the van again, but it wasn't behind him. He swore under his breath before he looked ahead and had to press the brakes quickly as the van cut in front of him.

Lewis glared as he saw the side door opening, and he put the car in reverse, gunning it, before turning left.

"Is that the van?" Sung-Rok asked as Lewis went up the street away from the van.

"They just cut right in front of me."

"I can see the license plate. I'll talk to you as soon as I have information." He said then the line went dead as Lewis drove back to take the highway.

By the time Lewis got back to the apartment, it'd been about an hour from when he'd told Seo-Yeon he would be home. He sighed as he pressed the button for the elevator and then grabbed his phone to make a quick call to let her know that he was back and would be in the apartment shortly.

"Hey, sorry, I was just on my way back and stopped to see Sung-Rok quickly. I'm downstairs now. So, I'll see you in a minute." Lewis said as the doors opened.

"Actually, I'm not at your place."

"Where are you at?" He frowned, standing inside the elevator as someone came in, and Lewis turned around to talk to Seo-Yeon.

"There was a slight emergency, so I came to the restaurant," Seo-Yeon replied.

"Fine, I'll start cooking, don't stay too late."

"You don't want to know what happened?"

"I trust that you took care of it, and will leave the manager to deal with it, so we can learn to trust him." He said, thinking it was better this way. He could calm down and cook, and then he wouldn't look too worried when she got back.

"Okay, well, I'll tell you when I get back. Love ya."

"Love you too." He said as he pressed the button for his floor and then put the phone away as the doors closed.

The man beside him turned around and pushed the stop button for the elevator as Lewis looked up.

"What's wrong?" he asked, trying hard not to sound too pissed off, as he'd not really been paying attention, and maybe there was a problem with the elevator that he'd not noticed.

"Is that how you should address your older brother, Lewis?" The man said, turning to face him as Lewis met his eyes.

"Peter…" He said, flabbergasted as he stared at his second eldest brother. "What are you doing here?"

"Don't you mean, how did I find you?" he asked with a smirk as he moved closer to Lewis.

At least, Lewis thought, he was taller and better built than Peter. Lewis was sure that he would knock him out if he wanted a fight.

"What do you want?" He asked defiantly.

"The family wants you back." He said with a slight shrug. "I just want you to stop impeding father's release from jail."

"Father?" He said and then laughed. "He doesn't deserve that title." He added, and then Peter struck him.

Leaning forward, Lewis felt the stabbing pain on his side. He remembered that pain from his teenage years. Peter's weapon of choice was a set of brass knuckles with a spike back then.

"Just so you know, we know everything about you. We've left you alone, thinking you would grow a conscience and leave Father alone, but we feel like we have to remind you what family means."

"Go to hell."

Peter's hand moved quickly, hitting Lewis twice on the side before his fist connected with Lewis's stomach.

"If you don't desist from this idea of justice, we'll make sure to take that beautiful head on your girl's shoulders. She'll probably look great lying next to your mother." He smirked before hitting Lewis right in the face and pushing the stop button for the elevator to move once more.

Lewis opened his mouth to say something, but as the doors opened and he leaned forward to try and stop Peter, he fell to the ground, losing consciousness.

Chapter eleven
Seo-Yeon

Seo-Yeon frowned, noticing the kitchen had closed, but a few people were still eating in the main dining room. After sweeping the room with her eyes one last time, she noticed the rather large man by the entrance and then walked toward him. She was sure that Lewis was stewing at home, too pissed off to call her.

"Sorry, we're closed for dinner." She said in English since the man looked like a tourist.

"What about a coffee?" He asked in an Australian accent as she smiled.

"I can do coffee, and we have some desserts left."

"Coffee will be fine."

"This way then." She said and walked to the table closest to the coffee station. "You sure I can't tempt you with one of the desserts." She asked

"No, but if you give me your number, maybe I'll get something equally sweet." He said in a lame way, but Seo-Yeon thought she should still be nice.

"I don't think that'll be good. My boyfriend is a wrestler." She told him. "Actually, he's Australian as well." She said to the man as she noticed the manager waving at her.

"I know," the man replied as Seo-Yeon turned to look at him and frowned.

"You know my boyfriend?"

"Lewis Parker, isn't it?" He asked, leaning against the chair.

"Yes."

"I knew him back in Sydney." He said casually. "That's why I decided to check out the place. Is he still here?"

"No, he's not, but he'll call you if you give me your name and number."

"Nah, I think he'll enjoy the surprise better."

"Okay, I'll be right back with your coffee." She said, walking back to the manager's station.

Seo-Yeon made sure that the bills were right before she gave them back to the manager and then returned to the table to hand the man the coffee. She wasn't sure why, but the guy was creeping her out. A few minutes later, he paid for his coffee and left, and she couldn't deny that she felt relief as she watched him go.

The rest of the shift was uneventful. Once the manager and the servers left, she returned to the office to make sure that she looked over the report before turning the computer off and then grabbed her bag and jacket.

Seo-Yeon made sure that everything was off, lights, gas line, and once she made sure that the till was locked, she turned off the air conditioning and the lights. She made a mental note to call the linen company when she heard a knock on the door's glass and turned around to greet him, thinking it was Lewis.

"Hey," the Australian man said, nodding as she froze in place. "Is Lewis picking you up?"

"Yes. He should be here soon." She said, glad that the manager had locked the front door.

"Is that right?" The man asked with a twisted smile that made Seo-Yeon's limbs feel heavier and her heart race faster.

"Yes, any minute now. So, you might be able to catch up with him tonight, after all."

"I guess so." He replied, his eyes hardening. The man stepped away from the glass door and took a few steps back near the elevator.

"Great," Seo-Yeon said, noticing the elevator light illuminating the hallway. At the same time, Simon and Seo-Joon stepped out of the lift.

Seo-Joon frowned, looking at the man who immediately got in the elevator, while Simon walked toward the front door.

"Why are you here so late?" Seo-Yeon asked, feeling undeniable relief as she saw her brother and Simon.

"Lewis had a bit of an accident, so we came to pick you up," Simon explained as she looked between them and saw the elevator doors closing.

"What do you mean? What sort of accident?" She asked, panicked as she looked between them and walked out of the restaurant.

"He's okay, but he was mugged when he arrived in his building," Simon explained as Seo-Joon frowned, looking at her.

"Mugged? How the hell? The building has CCTV!"

"Let's just get you to the hospital, Noona," Simon said, trying to take the keys from her, but Seo-Yeon closed her hand tighter around them.

"Yes, I just need to lock." She said, turning her attention to the door.

"Who was that?" Seo-Joon asked.

"I-I don't know. He said he knew Lewis and then came back after we closed." She said, feeling her body shiver before tears started to stream. "Why didn't one of you stay with him?"

"Sung-Rok Hyung is with him." Seo-Joon explained, reaching for the keys. "Did he hurt you?" Seo-Joon asked, worried as she shook her head.

"No." She said, giving him the keys. "I'm just—" She took a deep, shaky breath before tears streamed faster down her cheeks as Simon put an arm around her shoulders and handed her his handkerchief.

"He's fine, okay, Lewis Hyung is fine," Simon told her as they steered her to the elevator once Seo-Joon had locked the restaurant's doors.

"And Sung-Rok brought some more police officers to watch him," Seo-Joon added casually.

"Why? If it was a mugging?" she asked as the fear gave way to anger. "Why are there police officers guarding him?"

Seo-Joon swore under his breath and then took a deep breath in. "It seems that someone was following him."

"What? When? Who?" She asked, getting more upset as she held on tight to her purse.

"Lewis Hyung seems to think that someone from Australia was tailing him."

"His brothers?" Seo-Yeon asked, but she had reached Defcon one in seconds rather than being afraid.

"We don't know."

"It's gotta be them." She said, simply stepping out of the elevator as fast as possible. Seo-Joon and Simon both grabbed hold of each of her arms and then made her slow down.

"We don't know. That's why Sung-Rok is investigating," Seo-Joon told her in that authoritative older brother tone that drove her insane.

"Fine, whatever, I know what I know."

"Yes, and so do we. We can't jump to conclusions." Seo-Joon retorted, exasperated.

"They don't want him telling the Parole board to let that man rot in jail."

"It seems like it." Simon chimed in as they walked to his car.

"Apparently, he's very sick," Seo-Joon added.

"Like I said, he should rot in jail. He killed Lewis's mother."

"Hey, I'm not arguing with you, but this is what Lewis is dealing with now. You need to relax and make sure that you're not making him feel any worse than he feels right now." Seo-Joon said before he opened the door for her to get inside.

The look Seo-Joon gave her let her know that he wasn't expecting her to comply but was hoping that she would chill before they reached the hospital. And though she wanted to, the fact that someone had hurt her fiancé to try and silence him just pissed her off in ways that she couldn't describe.

Chapter twelve

Lewis

When his eyes opened again, Lewis wondered how long he'd dozed off since Seo-Joon and Simon were gone and had left Landry in their place. She looked a lot frailer than a few weeks earlier. Landry suddenly opened her eyes and stood up to help him as he tried to get the bed into a sitting position. She took the remote from his hand and then pressed the buttons to make him sit up.

"Are you comfortable now?"

"You're enjoying this, huh?"

"What?" Landry asked with a smirk. "Fussing over someone instead of having people fuss over me?" She asked and then gasped in mock surprise. "Never."

"Liar." He said and let out a soft chuckle before he winced as the pain spread through his stomach.

"Yeah, you should probably not laugh."

"Where's everyone?"

"Eomma is yelling at everyone who will listen to her, and Abeojim is talking to the doctors." She began to explain where their in-laws were as she fixed his pillow. "Simon and Seo-Joon went to pick Seo-Yeon up from the restaurant. Sung-Rokssi stationed a few police officers outside the door." She added.

"Oh, geez."

"Well, I never believed it, but it seems that you *are* a big deal." Landry teased him as Lewis lifted his arm and ran his hand through his hair.

"But Seo-Yeon is okay, right?"

"As far as I know," Landry told him and then took his hand in hers and squeezed it. "It's going to be fine." She said, letting go of his hand and then sighed. "I mean, this is just a walk in the park. At least you don't have to get chemo on top of being stabbed."

"I know, right?" He said deadpan as he stared at her. People often thought Landry was Lewis's sister since they were both blonde and had light blue eyes. After meeting her, he'd sort of adopted her as a sister. Both came from families who were really screwed up. They'd bonded over that, and now they had a family that smothered them with love.

"Do you also think it was your brothers?" Landry asked out of the blue as he took a deep breath to weigh in his response.

"I know it was. He was wearing a very nice suit and stabbed me with a smile."

"Oh, so you did see him." Landry bit her bottom lip.

"Yes, I'm just amazed that they deemed me that much of an enemy to look me up and come to warn me in person."

"But you already gave your letter, right?"

"I mailed it today."

"Wow, what timing." Landry frowned as Lewis nodded.

"The best timing." He replied as he looked at the monitor and then the cables.

"They said you can leave in a few days." She added when he didn't speak.

"So, what about you?"

"I'm fine."

"Bullshit."

"I am— I mean, this is a bit more taxing than before." She said with a shrug. "But I don't want any more treatment if this doesn't work." She whispered even though it was just her and Lewis. "My hair is all gone, my clothes are all baggy. What's the point of trying a new treatment?"

"What?" Lewis asked, flabbergasted as he watched her.

"I haven't told Seo-Joon yet." Landry's voice broke before her eyes met his. "But I can't keep putting him through this, and more than that, I don't think I can put myself through this again. This is the fourth time I've had to do chemo and operations and everything it entails. No, I just don't want to put myself through this again. I'm tired." Landry explained calmly because she'd made peace with this decision. "I've been given so much more than I ever dreamed of having. A husband, sister, mother, and father, they treat me like I mean something to them. Brothers." She said, offering him a half-smile before he took her hand in his and kissed it, hoping that she knew he supported her, even if he couldn't grasp all of it then. "You probably think I'm being selfish, or perhaps it *is* selfish, but I would like to die peacefully with him and our family." She pulled her hand away when she finished talking, probably thinking that Lewis would reject her.

He swallowed hard, so he wouldn't make her feel worse. It was clear that her mind was made up, but he knew the repercussions of her decision. "You're not selfish, Landry. And I don't think anyone will think you are selfish for not wanting to go through all of this again. We'll all be here for you, no matter your decision. We love you, and we want the best for you."

"I know, you guys, and Rosa, are the best siblings I could have ever asked for."

"Just," he hesitated and then sighed. "Don't wait too long to tell him. Seo-Joon wants the best for you, and if you think that's the best, he'll make it happen."

"I know." She nodded. "I just don't want to break his heart in the process." She replied as there was a knock on the door, and then it opened.

"Oh my gosh! Lewis." Seo-Yeon said, rushing in and throwing herself on top of him, hugging him tightly.

"You're going to kill me," Lewis said before he laughed again and winced.

"Where do you hurt?"

"Everywhere because you just threw yourself at me."

"I'm sorry, I'm sorry." She said and then climbed in the bed with him before looking at Landry. "Thank you."

"Don't mention it. It was great to bully someone for a change."

"As opposed to you being bullied?" Seo-Joon asked as Landry turned to look at him.

"You've not seen Seo-Yeon and Lorena in action." She whispered so only he could hear her, even though she was joking.

"If you're talking about Lorena and me, I will be ten times worse." Seo-Yeon joked, watching Seo-Joon and Simon walking out of the room with Landry. When the door closed, she turned to look at Lewis. "Do they know where your brothers are?"

"Sung-Rok seems to think that only Peter is here, but I don't know. Your description doesn't match Peter. I think one of the twins went to see you at the restaurant."

"Well, whoever it was, he creeped me out."

"So he saw you during service, right?" He asked, his brow wrinkling with concern.

"Yes, but he left. Then came back, that's when Seo-Joon Oppa and Simon came over to pick me up."

"That motherfucker." Lewis said as anger burned through him and Seo-Yeon frowned.

"I'm fine."

"It's not— I need to talk to Sung-Rok and let him know."

"I'll talk to him. You need to rest." She scolded him as she stood up.

"Be nice. Sung-Rok was the first at the scene and called the ambulance to help me straight away." Lewis said, looking at her.

"Of course, when have I not been nice to him?" Seo-Yeon asked as Lewis shook his head, knowing that was a can of worms. Seo-Yeon was sweet and a hard worker. However, that changed when someone she loved was hurt. Then, Seo-Yeon was a force not to be reckoned with, who would hunt down whoever she saw as a threat.

Chapter thirteen
Seo-Yeon

If it wasn't because they were in the middle of a long corridor that had several eyes on her, Seo-Yeon would have screamed. Still, she was really trying really hard to be level-headed. If anything, for Lewis's sake.

Sung-Rok glanced in her parents' direction before he spoke. "I know this is frustrating, but it's the best I got right now. We're trying to locate them. The van was rented through a third party, and there's no record of them entering the country."

"You must find them before they hurt Lewis again."

"It'll be good if you can give a statement at the precinct tomorrow," Sung-Rok told her. She followed his eyes to her parents, who were currently fussing over Landry and Seo-Joon.

"You will find them." She said, dismissing what he said.

"Seo-Yeon, this is very hard. I want to help, but I can't do much without any leads. I've already put out an A.P.B., so we can find them, but Lewis told me that they're masters of disguise and can move around like ghosts, without anyone noticing them."

"It's impossible. The man is blonde and is like seven feet tall. He's well built like Lewis. Do you think my fiancé is not memorable?"

"I didn't say that."

"Find him," Seo-Yeon said, walking toward her parents.

"I hope you didn't bite Sung-Rok Hyung's head off," Seo-Joon said, looking at his sister.

"I didn't. I just told him to do his job."

"He's trying, but it's very hard. There's no CCTV footage in Lewis's building and nothing in the cars parked near the building. I guess he's not going to find much at the Lotte Tower either."

"We have a camera. I'll make sure to give him the footage tomorrow." Seo-Yeon replied. "Thanks for staying with Lewis. I hope he wasn't annoying because he usually is impossible when he's sick, so I can imagine if he was stroppy."

"He was fine," Landry replied with a tired smile.

"We're going to go, Landry needs to rest, and I have to get up early tomorrow morning," Seo-Joon said, looking at his sister. "Maybe tell Sung-Rok that you have the CCTV footage before he goes." He said before saying goodbye to their parents and Seo-Yeon.

Once she was alone with her mother, they walked back to the bedroom to find Lewis sleeping. Instead of staying inside, they returned to the hallway and sat down.

"You look tired. You should go too." Her mother said as Seo-Yeon shook her head.

"I won't be able to sleep."

"Go inside and lie down on the sofa. I'll stay here."

"No, Eomma, you should go home and rest. You have work tomorrow."

"I'm fine." She said with a serious expression as she looked at the wall in front of her.

"I'm sorry," Seo-Yeon said with a sniffle.

"Why?" She asked with a frown. "You didn't stab Lewis." Mrs. Shim said, wrapping an arm around Seo-Yeon's shoulder and then sighed. "Don't be silly."

"I know you are all worried about Landry as well. And this—"

"This was nothing. He's fine, and everyone's fine. We just need to rest. Is that why you're crying now." She told her as she cupped her cheeks in her hands. "Nothing is going to happen to him or you or Landry."

"You can't make such a promise."

"Well, you and Lewis will be fine." She said in a sad tone as she let go of Seo-Yeon's cheeks.

"Landry will be fine too," Seo-Yeon said with a determined look. "Appa and Seo-Joon will work hard and help her, so she's okay."

"Of course, they will." Her mother replied, looking at her. "Go rest. I'll be here if you need me."

"Fine," Seo-Yeon said, looking at her and then smiled. "Eomma— I love you." She said, kissing her mother's cheek.

"I love you too, Seo-Yeon… just go now."

Seo-Yeon stood up and then walked back into the room before climbing in the bed as best as she could cuddle Lewis.

The following day, Seo-Yeon helped Lewis go to the bathroom and have a quick shower before returning to the restaurant to look at the CCTV footage. Sung-Rok insisted on meeting her there even though he'd assigned a police officer to escort her around Seoul.

After she looked through the footage, Sung-Rok recorded the evidence and thanked her but didn't leave. Seo-Yeon frowned, wondering if he was still annoyed at her. She knew how much Seo-Joon, Lewis, and Simon loved him. Sometimes, she could go overboard, but she hadn't meant to be mean or disrespectful.

"Yes?" She asked, but her voice sounded aggravated rather than neutral. *I guess I should apologize for this as well.*

"I know Lewis already sent his letter to the Parole board… but maybe you should just advise him not to get involved anymore."

"What? Are you kidding me?" She asked, her voice rising several decibels.

"Seo-Yeonssi, I know how much everything that happened has affected Lewis. And I also know he's doing this because he believes it's his way to protect his mother. But his mother is gone, and I doubt that she would want him to keep on putting a target on his back over this."

"That man should rot in jail." Seo-Yeon spat out furiously.

"Seo-Yeonssi, I understand the pain that Lewis went through. Believe me when I say that I know how much he suffered. But it's time for him to let go. You have a full life ahead. The two of you are about to get married. And not to sound preachy like Simon, but you don't want to take this anger and hatred into your marriage. You have a life ahead of you that can be full of love and laughter and very little thought for someone so wicked who has nothing to do with Lewis anyway."

Seo-Yeon stared at him and then looked away, taking a deep breath in. She understood what he was saying, but she still wanted some justice for Lewis. All that his father put him through, there should be a way for him to pay.

"Do you want to be right or win?"

"What?" She blinked, turning to face him again.

"Do you want to be right or win? If you want to be right, you'll help him move on. If you want to win, then you'll want him to continue to pursue this, and Lewis's dad will be out in less than a year or two, anyway."

"We're not vengeful people," Seo-Yeon said, trying hard to sound calm and failing. "Look at what his brothers have done to him. He's in hospital. He could have died."

"Could have, but he didn't," Sung-Rok replied. "We're going to protect him to the best of our abilities." He said, and Seo-Yeon thought he was giving up because he couldn't convince her to tell Lewis to drop it. "I'll make sure that we keep this in file." He said, shaking the USB in his hand and then nodded. "I'll see you later," Sung-Rok added, walking away.

Seo-Yeon frowned, wondering if he was right. After all, she and Lewis had nothing to do with Lewis's family. It had always saddened her that he couldn't have a relationship with his many siblings or the nephews and nieces that he surely had. More than that, Lewis missed Australia but never wanted to say it out loud, and Seo-Yeon wondered how much it hurt that he was in a self-imposed exile. She sighed, closing the window in the computer, and then pulled up the Quick Books app so she could start working on the payroll.

Chapter fourteen,

Lewis

After sitting down on the couch, Lewis glanced around the room as Seo-Joon and Simon split chores. One was ordering food on his phone, and the other was making sure that the letters were stacked neatly on the desk.

"You guys need to stop. I'm fine." Lewis said when they both returned to the living room and sat near Lewis.

"Of course, but you shouldn't overdo it. Even if the stab wound isn't deep, you should take it easy." Seo-Joon said in what Lewis believed was his doctor's tone.

"Sure, sir." Lewis teased him and then leaned against the couch. "I do appreciate the fact that I can sleep a bit more. It's been like two years since I've been sleeping only four hours a night."

"You really need to take better care of yourself, Hyung," Simon told him as he checked his phone. "Food will be here soon. I ordered your favorite."

"Japchae?" Lewis asked as Simon nodded.

"With rice, I also added soondae just for you," Simon said, turning his nose.

"I still don't get why you don't like it. It's delicious." Lewis said, referring to the black pudding dish. He liked it better than the black pudding he'd known growing up. The glass noodles somehow gave it a different texture, and it was just better overall.

"Yes, and you can enjoy it all on your own."

"And you two call yourselves Korean." He teased Simon and Seo-Joon before handing the remote control to Seo-Joon.

"So, what did Father Matteo want?" Seo-Joon asked.

"Oh, you know, he came to check on me and pray with me." He shrugged. Lewis ran a hand through his hair and then took the remote control back after Seo-Joon had turned on the tv and found a channel with a variety show on.

"That's nice of him," Seo-Joon replied.

"Yeah, well, I think he knows how stressed Seo-Yeon has been. It was nice, especially with all the stuff going on with Lorena and Simon's building site."

"Hey, we're not stressing him out," Simon said, looking up from the phone and then putting it in his pocket. "There's just a lot of forms for them to sign, and the government isn't making it easy on us either."

"I told you to talk to my contact, but no, you had to go and do it on your own," Lewis said flatly.

"Hyung, I'm sorry, but the foundation has its own contacts. I did try." Simon pouted.

"Did you talk to Sung-Rok Hyung about your brother?" Seo-Joon asked while Lewis took a deep breath and shifted on the couch.

"There's nothing for me to do now, guys." This had most likely rubbed onto Seo-Yeon, who now felt paranoid about him dropping his current pursuit to keep his father behind bars. "Sung-Rok is doing his job, and we all have either police escorts or bodyguards." He shrugged.

"Hey, we understand." Simon started. "But maybe you should drop the appeal. Your father served a long time, and he's so far away. Perhaps if you just forgive him—"

"Would you be able to forgive such a thing?" Lewis asked as anger shook his voice.

"No, I don't think I could," Simon admitted looking at the floor.

"I know everyone's worried, but I believe this is a one-off. They've probably buggered off to Australia already, and this won't happen again."

"I do hope you're right," Seo-Joon said severely. "You can't put my sister in danger like that, Hyung."

"I didn't mean to. This is why I've not been back to Australia."

"Yes, but it didn't happen there. It's happened here." Seo-Joon said in full older brother mode.

Lewis took a deep breath in understanding Seo-Joon's reservation and his anger. He'd brought his own problems into their family and put Seo-Yeon in danger. "I'm really sorry about that."

"It's not that," Seo-Joon replied cuttingly. "You need to think about you and Seo-Yeon now. The past has no place in this new life of yours. Isn't that why you ran away and came here?"

Lewis felt the frustration from Seo-Joon as their eyes met. He felt terrible but also embarrassed. Among his friends, Lewis's family was the most embarrassing one. He cast his eyes down to the floor and then shrugged. "I know you're right."

"You need to protect my sister."

"I will," Lewis said though he wasn't sure how to do that and still protect his mother's memory.

Lewis's phone went off when Simon went to get the door, as the food had arrived. He frowned, looking at the name on the screen, and picked it up.

"Yes, Sung-Rok Hyung?" Lewis asked.

"Lewis, we got them." He said simply as Lewis's grip on the phone became tighter.

"I beg your pardon?"

"We arrested your brothers. There were actually two of them trying to board a private jet."

"Where are they?"

"They're at the precinct. Come by when you can."

After hanging up, Lewis stared at the phone and then looked at Seo-Joon and Simon. "They're at the police station."

"Who?" Simon asked.

"My brothers."

"Let's eat quickly," Seo-Joon said. Lewis's stomach growled in agreement, even though Lewis had been wondering if he could just drive to the police station on an empty stomach.

***

Seo-Joon and Simon followed Lewis into the police station and then walked down the hallway to the waiting area where they'd been told to wait. Before Lewis stood up and looked at the vending machine, Seo-Joon paced around, and Simon answered a few emails. He could feel the fear in the pit of his stomach. Could he really see this through? After all, he'd always tried to have a relationship with his siblings, but this had crossed the line. Tailing him, scaring Seo-Yeon, stabbing him, Lewis shook his head slightly as he willed himself not to think anymore. It was necessary to relinquish his feelings. He had to approach this with a clear mind. After all, he no longer belonged to the family. His siblings had always stated they hated him. It was about time for him to stop wishing things would be different. He had to treat them like strangers.

Simon apologized when his phone went off and sighed as he answered. Lewis and Seo-Joon both glanced his way as he seemed to be getting paler every second that ticked on.

"What's wrong?" Lewis and Seo-Joon asked at the same time.

"Lorena's at the hospital. She's spotting." He said, frowning as Seo-Joon placed a hand on his shoulder.

"It's going to be fine. Go. I'll take a taxi home." Lewis said, looking at them.

"Are you sure?" Seo-Joon asked as Lewis gave him an are-you-kidding-me-now look.

"Of course, yes, let's go," Seo-Joon said, leading Simon out of the waiting room as Lewis sat down and waited.

A few seconds later, Sung-Rok knocked on the side of the room and smiled at Lewis. "You ready?"

"As ready as I'll ever be." He sighed, standing up and following him.

Sung-Rok walked with Lewis to the room just outside the interview room and then glanced at him. "I told you, you didn't need to come over, but since you're here." He said, looking at him. Lewis noticed four policemen and two men he recognized from the telly inside his brothers' interrogation room. One was an American lawyer who had been in Korea for over a decade, and the other was a New Zealand lawyer who'd been involved in a few high-profile cases. He sighed, wondering if they were connected to his brothers or it'd been a fluke. 'Someone rang them up since your brothers don't speak Korean." Sung-Rok finally explained when Lewis leaned closer to the glass. "Figures."

"They'll both stay in jail while we investigate," Sung-Rok explained and then turned when the door opened. "Do you want to talk to them before starting the next hour of interviews?"

"Yes," he said, nodding.

Sung-Rok nodded, escorting him out of the room and around the hallway to the entrance of the interview room. He opened the door, letting Lewis walk in first, before stepping behind him.

The two lawyers looked up from their notes as they looked between Sung-Rok and Lewis.

"Brother." The smirk on Joshua's face didn't surprise Lewis in the least. He sighed, walking over, but Sung-Rok stopped him from getting closer.

"I didn't think you would run scared, but here you are," Peter said and then glanced at Joshua. "Don't you think he looks like a little pussy?"

"I don't know why you're trying to rile me up," Lewis said. "I'm not the one sitting in jail." He smirked, causing them to give him aggravated looks.

"We're going to be gone soon." Peter shrugged.

"Didn't you break parole rules?" Lewis asked cocking his head to the side as he met his brothers' eyes. They'd both served jail time, just like their older brother Caleb. "I mean, you were allowed to leave jail with a certain set of rules. and here you are, committing yet more crimes, in South Korea."

"I guess you're feeling a lot more courageous since you have a few cops around," Peter said, his blue eyes fixing on Lewis. "We're not staying here. I can assure you that."

"Yeah, I don't think you know how this works. Especially after you've gotten in hot water with South Korea… I wonder if they'll send you to jail for ten years or maybe just eight." Lewis replied, looking at him. "I'll see you in court." He said, turning on his heels and walking out of the room before taking a deep breath to steady his anger.

"Come with me, so you can give the witness statement to the lead investigator. I don't think your testimony from a few days ago when you were heavily sedated was good enough." Sung-Rok told him as he led him down the corridor.

Lewis stopped, his hand balling into a fist before looking over his shoulder to the closed door.

"What's wrong?"

"This is the last time," Lewis said before meeting Sung-Rok's eyes. "I'll fly to take some flowers to my mother's grave because no one in the family ever visits, and no one pays their respects. Just one of my friends. He does it all. However, her birthday is next month." He said, saddened by it. He'd allowed his father and siblings to stop him from doing just that for years. "After they're jailed, I'll just forget that they're all still alive somewhere." He explained as his eyes fixed on the floor. "We were never close. I was the youngest, the son of another woman… but I still always tried to be a good brother."

Lewis felt his voice shaking in anger and pain. "All the scars on my body are what's left of my attempts at being a good brother. Every cigarette burn, every stab wound… I'll forget all of it."

Sung-Rok sighed as he patted Lewis's back and offered him a half-smile. "You have a full life ahead of you, a family that loves you, sisters, brothers, and good parents." He said, nodding. "It's time to bury the past. They'll be taken care of for breaking the law. Let me do my work, and just be happy." He added as Lewis stared at him and then looked toward the end of the hallway.

"I'm going to try really hard to forget." He promised, walking toward the front door of the precinct.

"I'm sure you'll get there," Sung-Rok told him as Lewis nodded.

"Thanks for everything," he said sincerely.

"Hey, I'm your Hyung. I'm always going to be here for you and Seo-Yeon." He said, giving him a quick hug as Lewis hugged him back.

"Talk to you later." He added before he walked toward the street in search of a taxi so he could go to the hospital to make sure that Lorena was okay.

Chapter fifteen

Seo-Yeon

Seo-Yeon and her best friend Bom Hyuk met in one of the hallways as Seo-Yeon rushed to maternity to check on Lorena. The two friends took the elevator together and moved to its back as some more people got in.

"So, what happened?" Bom-Hyuk asked, running a hand through her hair before leaning against the back of the elevator.

"I'm not sure," Seo-Yeon replied since she'd only gotten a text from Seo-Joon to come to the hospital because he had to pick Landry up from her chemo.

"Is Seo-Joon here too?" Bom-Hyuk asked as Seo-Yeon turned to look at her friend and then nodded.

"He's got to pick Landry up as well."

"Oh, how is she doing?"

"She's nearly done with this round of chemo."

"Hopefully, it'll be okay, at least for a while."

"I don't know. Everything just keeps on piling, and … We need to catch up later." She said as the elevator dinged and the people in front of them got out.

"Of course, when you can."

"It's just so crazy," Seo-Yeon said as the doors closed.

"Hey, we've been best friends since probably conception. I'm always here when you need me." She said, ensuring her lanyard was around her neck, and Seo-Yeon smiled at her.

"You've not changed at all." She chuckled as she moved to the front of the elevator with her.

"Well, that's good, or we wouldn't be friends," Bom-Hyuk replied.

"True," Seo-Yeon said as the doors opened, and she took a deep breath in.

Bom-Hyuk slid her arm through hers and then nodded. "I have some time."

"No, you're busy." Seo-Yeon protested, walking out of the elevator with Bom-Hyuk, who didn't let go of her arm.

"I'm never too busy for you." Bom-Hyuk offered her a grin and then took a deep breath of her own. "Let's go see your friend." She said in a positive tone, though Seo-Yeon knew that Bom-Hyuk hurt every time she saw Seo-Joon.

Growing up, Seo-Joon and Bom-Hyuk had been inseparable. They had been good friends until Bom-Hyuk and Seo-Yeon bonded over not being allowed to join a boys' soccer team, which was the only soccer team. Seo-Yeon's mom and Bom's mother decided to do their own thing and got sponsors to form an all-girls team, eventually beating the boys' team. And when both girls started to crush on boys, Seo-Yeon had kept the secret of how much Bom-Hyuk really liked Seo-Joon. It was just too bad that he'd never seen her as anything other than a little sister. Seo-Yeon loved Landry and Seo-Joon, but her heart often broke for her friend, who was never interested in other guys.

"Hey, I didn't know if I would see you today," Seo-Joon said as he smiled at Bom. "Your brother just texted me about the class reunion. Why aren't you going? Seo-Yeon is totally dragging Lewis to it."

"Oh, I don't know if I am," Seo-Yeon said as she glared daggers at Seo-Joon.

"She'll totally go. And you'll probably have fun." He said to Bom as she blushed slightly.

"I don't know. I have a really crazy schedule now." Bom-Hyuk replied, staring at Seo-Joon before forcing her eyes away. "How's Lorena?"

"Simon's inside with her, but I don't really know anything more."

"I'll go," Bom-Hyuk said, and then Seo-Yeon grinned at her taking her hand in hers and squeezing it. 'Don't worry." She told Seo-Yeon and then smiled at Seo-Joon. "It's always nice seeing you." She nodded and then walked toward the locked doors, waving her card near the reader for the doors to open.

Seo-Yeon turned once more to look at her brother and then frowned. "You need more sleep."

"Landry wasn't feeling very well last night. She hardly slept."

"I understand, but you need to take care of yourself as well." She said as he checked his phone.

"She still has ten minutes left upstairs, so I'll wait with you for Bom."

"Great way to change subjects." She said, her voice dripping in sarcasm.

"Hey, you have your abilities. I have mine." He joked, sitting beside her on the bench near the door.

"How was it at the police station?" Seo-Yeon asked him, and he shrugged.

"I think Sung-Rok will get through Lewis."

"I don't know." Seo-Yeon bit her bottom lip, her eyes on the red and white painting on the doors.

"It'll be fine. I promise."

"You can't promise that." She said, turning to face him. "This isn't something you can fix. Lewis needs to take the decision. Do we never set foot in Australia? Do we just forget about his family and go?"

"Well, they're going to be jailed, according to Sung-Rok. He's sure of it. They came illegally through a private jet and moved around, hiring convicts."

"I don't really care if they get jailed here or in Australia. I just want Lewis to stop hurting because of them."

"You can't wave a magic wand and do that. But you can just let him deal with his feelings right now." He said, looking at her. "It must be horrible to think that your brothers, with whom you've only ever tried to reconnect, don't care for you the same way. And that they would go to a foreign country just to intimidate you—" he let his voice trail off and then stood up as Bom walked out the doors.

"Hey," Bom-Hyuk said, slightly breathless as she stopped in front of them. "She's fine, and the baby's fine. They're monitoring her. I think the doctor will make her stay in bed until the baby's born, but don't quote me on it." She added as Seo-Yeon saw Lewis walking toward them. "Simon said he'll be out in a bit." She said as her phone began ringing. "I'll see you soon. But if you need me, you know I'm a text away." She told Seo-Yeon before waving at Seo-Joon. "Fighting!" She said, stepping inside the elevator.

"That's a relief," Seo-Joon said to Seo-Yeon as she nodded.

"I'm glad that the baby's fine. Lorena's been so stressed about the pregnancy." She said when she noticed Lewis walking toward them and waved at him.

Lewis walked the rest of the way to them and then sighed. "Is she leaving because of me?" Lewis asked Seo-Yeon as he joined her and Seo-Joon when Bom-Hyuk walked away.

"Yes, she still hates you for teasing her about her non-existent crush on me." Seo-Joon teased him as his phone dinged. "That's gotta be Landry. I'll see you both later." He said, walking toward the elevators.

"Everyone always leaves when I arrive."

"That's not true. I'm still here." Seo-Yeon smirked, looking at him.

"And thank God for that." He said, nodding. "I have news."

"News?" She asked, blinking for a moment before she arched an eyebrow. "Did they get charged?"

"Oh, no, not about that," Lewis said with a smile.

"So… what then?"

"I booked four plane tickets. Tickets for you and me and your parents, so we can get married in Australia."

Chapter sixteen

Lewis

Lewis watched Seo-Yeon process the words he had spoken. Her silence was somewhat unnerving, so he took her hands in his and squeezed them tight. The reaction Lewis hoped for never came. His eyes darted to the people walking about the hospital before returning them to Seo-Yeon. Several minutes before she spoke again, made Lewis overthink his impulsive decision to buy the plane tickets.

"You did, what?" She asked, confused.

"We're going to Australia. I'll take you to see Sydney and where my mother is buried. And we'll marry there before returning home to Seoul." He explained as Seo-Yeon bit her lip.

"Are you feeling okay?" She asked, her eyes full of concern.

"Never better."

"But your family…" her voice trailed off before he pressed his lips against her forehead.

"You're my family, the only family I care about."

"Okay, but the rest of your siblings are there." She reminded him.

"I don't care. I don't want to get hung up on that. I just want to show you my old place and watch you walk across the beach on a tiny bikini." He wiggled his eyebrows as she pulled her hands away and smacked his shoulder.

"I mean, I don't— I'm not opposed to this." She told him as he leaned closer and kissed her forehead.

"Good, because we're going."

Seo-Yeon cupped his cheeks in her hands and smiled at him. "Very well, so you'll have to tell my brother and the others because I'm pretty sure that they'll all get offended if we don't tell them."

"Of course." He said, nodding and then biting his lip.

"Oh, is there more to this?" Seo-Yeon said, letting go of his cheeks when he straightened up a bit more.

"I want to see my father as well."

"Are you sure?"

Lewis looked at the floor, gathering his thoughts. Seo-Yeon closed the space between them, but he stopped her from getting close to him.

"I need closure, real closure." He began as she met his eyes.

"Then we'll go get it." Seo-Yeon offered him a half-smile, then kissed his lips tenderly.

"I want to be a good dad."

"I know."

"I've wondered…" his voice cracked as he looked past her, feeling his eyes pooling. "I've wondered if all the anger in me if that's why God—"

"No," Seo-Yeon said in a firm tone as she locked eyes with him.

"God is love. God doesn't punish."

"If I were better and not so angry," Lewis said in a barely audible whisper as Seo-Yeon wrapped her arms around him.

"You are a good man, Lewis. If you weren't, I wouldn't give you the time of day." She joked softly before kissing his cheek. "And I'm a good woman. This is just something that happened because of biology."

"I'm sorry," Lewis said, feeling like a weight had lifted from his shoulders, but pain and tears were aftermaths. He pulled her closer to him, his body shaking as the tears streaked his cheeks.

"You don't have to apologize," Seo-Yeon said against his shoulder as she wrapped her arms tighter around him.

"I do."

Seo-Yeon cupped his cheeks in her hands again and looked straight into his eyes before offering a warm smile. "Then I accept your apology, and I also apologize for not having a workable uterus."

"That's not funny."

"No, neither is you apologizing for stuff you can't control." She said, kissing his lips tenderly.

"Is this a bad time?" Simon's voice cut through Lewis as he pulled away from Seo-Yeon and shook his head.

"No, how's Lorena?" Seo-Yeon asked quickly as she turned her body around to face him.

"She's okay, worried." He said, putting his hands in his pockets.

"Will it be easy for her to take time off and do the whole bed rest thing?" Seo-Yeon asked, and then when Simon stared at her confused, she cleared her throat. "Bom-Hyuk told us."

"Oh. Yes, well, Min-Young will talk to people, and I guess some of the things she was going to do will be canceled. We might have to pay some penalties for the cancellations. I don't really want to think about that."

"Don't talk about it then," Lewis told him and then patted his back.

"It's going to be fine. I texted Father Matteo, so he'll probably swing by later on. I guess he's still busy with mass."

"Thanks, Hyung."

"Hey, we're family," Lewis told him and then heard someone calling Simon's name.

"Sarah!" Simon said, rushing over to his twin sister and picking her up. He hugged her.

"Did you call her?" Lewis frowned, turning to look at Seo-Yeon. "Even if I had, the last thing I knew was that she was in London."

"Ow," Sarah frowned as Simon put her down.

"What's wrong?" He asked as Lewis and Seo-Yeon walked over to them.

"In the whole, I gotta get to Seoul rush. I fell and bruised my ribs." Sarah said before she looked at Lewis. "Hey, you guys."

"Hey, you guys? What? Did I stop being Oppa? When did I stop being Oppa?" He asked as she rubbed the side of her body.

"Since you're more of an ahjussi, I don't want to insult you." Sarah teased him, using the word that best described men over a certain age before Seo-Yeon gave her a half hug.

"Did I hurt you?" Simon asked as he moved closer to her.

"Well, my ribs are bruised, and you just squeezed me," she explained as Simon frowned.

"I'm sorry, I didn't know. You should be more careful." Simon scolded her gently.

"Hey, how are you guys? I got you coffee," Tae-Hyung said, walking toward them with two cups of coffee. Once he reached her, he handed her one of the cups of coffee.

"What? What are you doing here?" Simon asked Tae-Hyung, narrowing his eyes, before looking from Tae-Hyung back to Sarah then back to Tae-Hyung.

"Oh, well, Tae-Hyung was in London, and we met at the airport. I told him about Lorena, so he offered to escort me here." Sarah explained before taking a sip from the coffee cup.

Whatever Simon was thinking there, it was clear that he was most displeased about the recent turn of events. He opened his mouth several times but finally closed it without saying a word.

"So, we were going to go. Maybe you two want to spend some time together." She said clearly, meaning Sarah and Simon as her eyes fixed on Tae-Hyung and Lewis took it to mean that he should also help make Tae-Hyung leave. Even if he'd apologized to Lorena, Simon was still pretty pissed off at what he'd done.

"Well, that was very kind, Tae-Hyung, but we can take it from here," Simon said.

"Is Lorena okay and the baby?" Tae-Hyung asked Simon, clearly taking him aback when Simon opened and closed his mouth again. Tae-Hyung's tone had been of genuine concern, and Simon was obviously touched.

"They're both fine, thank you," Simon said in a friendlier tone.

"I'm glad they're fine," Tae-Hyung said in a sincere tone, but it was clear Simon wasn't going to say anything else.

"You know what, I didn't bring my car. Did you drive here?" Lewis asked Tae-Hyung.

"Actually, yes, we picked up my car at the airport because I didn't want my manager coming all the way and alerting the fans." He said as Lewis nodded.

"Great, so you don't mind giving me a lift?"

"No, it's fine—" Tae-Hyung nodded. "It'll be nice to catch up."

"All right, we'll see you later," Lewis said, patting Tae-Hyung's back to steer him toward the elevator.

Seo-Yeon waved at Lewis before she and Simon started walking back closer to the doors, but Sarah stood rooted to the spot.

"I'll see you later," Tae-Hyung said to her as Lewis walked in the elevator and held the doors open for him.

Lewis looked between them and sighed. This was going to be bad if Sarah and Tae-Hyung were actually dating. Simon was a good guy, maybe sometimes naïve, but he wouldn't let anyone play with his sister's feelings. Lewis wasn't sure that Tae-Hyung had any sort of good intentions when it came to Sarah though he was going to take the time to ask him as they drove home.

 Tae-Hyung stood beside him inside the elevator and sighed softly as the doors closed. Lewis leaned back against the wall and then turned his head toward Tae-Hyung. "I do hope you know what you're getting into."

"Hyung, you don't know the half of it," Tae-Hyung replied as the doors closed.

Chapter seventeen

Seo-Yeon

After Simon and Sarah went inside, Seo-Yeon leaned against the wall and scrolled down through her emails on the phone. She wasn't sure how long she'd been waiting when Sarah joined her once more.

"Still here, Unnie?" Sarah asked when Seo-Yeon looked at her.

"Of course, I guess you need a ride."

"Oh, well, I could have just taken a cab. My luggage is still in Tae-Hyung's car."

"So, you and Tae-Hyung have become close?" Seo-Yeon asked as they started to walk to the elevator.

"I guess you can say that. I mean, we're friends now. Before, I was just the annoying twin sister of his bandmember." She explained.

"Friends?"

"Oh," Sarah frowned, watching her. "Should I not bother with him because of what happened between him and Lorena?" She said, shrugging as Seo-Yeon pushed the button to call for the elevator.

"I'm not saying that. I'm not in any position to be mean to him. Lorena has forgiven Tae-Hyung, and accepted her own culpability in the matter since she did have a fling with him."

"Therefore, you're not going to judge me based on my new friend, right?"

"I guess so." She replied, defeated as Sarah smiled brightly at her.

"So, is everything okay with Lewis and his brothers?" Sarah asked, concerned.

"Yes, they were arrested, and there's enough evidence so that they can't get away with having attacked him. They broke several other laws too and hired some thugs." She shook he head. "It's like a bloody bad movie." She said as they stepped into the elevator.

"You must have been beside yourself with worry," Sarah said as she stood beside her.

"It was hard, but mostly, I felt bad for not believing Lewis. He'd always been so adamant that his family was full of lowlifes. I just thought he was saying it because he was still so angry at them for taking their father's side."

"Well, I'm glad he wasn't badly hurt or you."

"I'm fine," Seo-Yeon said, nodding. "Everything okay with you and the model?"

"Oh…" Sarah's voice trailed off as the doors opened and a few people got inside the elevator. "I don't think we'll be seeing each other anymore. I can't deal with all the modeling stuff." Sarah said, playing with the strap of her purse.

"I see," Seo-Yeon said and then looked toward the numbers as they lit up. "Are you back for good then?"

"No, I like my life in England. Gracie and Henry are just so amazing. I'll have even more responsibility in the next few months because she's pregnant. She wants me to take over when she goes on maternity leave. Not too shabby, right? Once she goes on maternity leave, I'll officially be the President." She said and then shook her head as a giggle escaped her. "It sounds ridiculous, but I'm quite happy about the title."

"Wow, that's really good, Sarah." She said sincerely and then frowned. "I guess you won't be able to come to Australia with us."

"What? What do you mean?" She asked as they left the elevator. Seo-Yeon took a deep breath and then braced herself to explain the whole trip to Sydney. "Lewis wants us to get married in Australia, and he also wants everyone to be there if possible."

"Destination wedding? Please, count me in."

"How much holiday time do you have accumulated?" Seo-Yeon teased her. "You just started work with Gracie."

"Oh, we don't have that sort of contract. I will be running the show in a few months when she is on maternity leave. Trust me, she's really flexible, and if it's now, she won't even say no. She basically owes me." Sarah grinned as they walked together to the parking lot.

"You landed a good job then."

"I guess," Sarah replied as Seo-Yeon searched for her keys. "This is probably a nosy question, but are you guys really looking into adoption?"

"Yes, Mom and Dad seemed to be on board, and we don't care about people asking stupid questions."

"Oh, you know those are bound to happen, and a lot." Sarah nodded. "But that's really good." She told her.

"Well, Lewis is sure that we'll find our kids out there."

"Really?" Sarah asked, unable to hide her surprise. "He's really grown, eh?"

"He's matured a bit." Seo-Yeon agreed as she unlocked the car doors with the car fob key.

"How many kids do you want to adopt?"

"I don't know, I think we should start with one, but you know Lewis's special." She joked. "He wants a whole football team."

"British?"

"Australian Rules." Seo-Yeon watched her and then sighed.

"Twenty-two."

"Oh, hell no." Sarah climbed in the car and then pulled at the seat belt before wincing.

"Did you really go to the hospital?" Seo-Yeon asked as she looked at her.

"I'm fine. They said it's just bruised, not broken."

Seo-Yeon kept her eyes on hers while Sarah tried to pull at the seat belt again. When Seo-Yeon saw her wince again, she bit her lip once the belt went across her lap. Seo-Yeon kept her eyes on Sarah, thinking about a time when she too had bruised ribs and even a few broken bones. Memories of a worse time in her life flashed across her eyes. Of course, she'd hid it from the family, but Lewis had sussed it out.

"Sarah, what really happened?" She asked in a sisterly tone, her eyes trying to look right in Sarah's eyes.

"Nothing, I'm fine," Sarah replied dismissively as she looked away.

"Sarah—"

"I fell." She said curtly as her eyes turned to the window.

"I used to fall too a long time ago," Seo-Yeon said, turning the engine on before she pulled out of the parking lot. "Remember? You and Simon were so young." As the car rolled to a stop, she looked at the traffic.

"We weren't that young, Unnie. We were eighteen." She said, and Seo-Yeon nodded.

"You and Simon noticed straight away."

"It wasn't like that," Sarah said defensively.

"Is this why you aren't very close to Lorena? Did she find out?"

"Unnie—"

"Lorena has experienced this crap too," Seo-Yeon said, ignoring her pleading tone.

"I didn't want to make a big deal. It wasn't that bad. Tae-Hyung stopped him as soon as he tried to—" Sarah stopped talking when Seo-Yeon's phone rang. "You should pick up."

Seo-Yeon frowned, looking at the screen next to the steering wheel. Seo-Joon's name flashed as she moved her hand to push the button to answer the call through the steering wheel system.

"What's wrong, Seo-Joon?"

"Where are you at?" He asked as Seo-Yeon looked ahead.

"I'm taking Sarah to her apartment."

"Can you pass by the house?" Seo-Yeon felt the emptiness in her stomach stretch. Why was he asking her to go to the house? He'd just been at the hospital. Had something happened to Landry?"

"Sure," she replied, trying to sound normal. "I'll be there soon," Seo-Yeon said as he hung up.

"Do you think something's wrong with Landry?" Sarah asked worriedly.

"I hope not," Seo-Yeon said before she made a right turn to take the highway. "Sarah— did Spencer try to hit you?"

Sarah let a soft sigh escape her before she turned to look at Seo-Yeon. "Yes."

"And Tae-Hyung stopped him?"

"Yes," Sarah said after a pause. "He beat him up."

"Good." Seo-Yeon nodded. "Sarah," she said, glancing at her. "I'm always here when you want to talk about it." She said, getting off the highway.

"I know, Unnie. Thank you." Sarah replied while Seo-Yeon nodded as she approached the entrance to Sarah's street.

"Anytime, anywhere," Seo-Yeon said, trying to reassure her.

"Yes," Sarah nodded as the car stopped in front of her building. "Thanks for the lift."

"Anytime, anywhere," Seo-Yeon told her again before Sarah met her eyes and nodded in acknowledgment of the promise. She then climbed out of the car.

***

Seo-Yeon walked up to the door and knocked, her heart beating faster than before as she wondered if something was wrong with Landry. She closed her eyes for a moment willing her heart to calm down before the door opened.

"Hey, what's up?" She asked Seo-Joon, who stepped aside for her to walk inside the house.

"Landry wanted to see you."

"Me?" She asked as she walked with him toward the living room and then smiled at Landry. "Hey," she said as she looked from Landry to Seo-Joon.

"I have a little thing for you," Landry said, visibly weaker than before, but she told herself it was probably side effects from the chemo.

"What is it?"

Landry nodded, and Seo-Joon moved to the coffee table and then picked up a box giving it to Seo-Yeon.

Seo-Yeon took it and then sat on the sofa next to Landry. She opened the box, which was the size of a shoebox, and gasped when she noticed the beautiful shoes inside it. They were silver and looked like someone had added metallic lace to them. The whole effect made it look like they were designed for a princess. "Did you make this?"

Landry nodded. "I'm just glad I could finish them before the chemo started."

"Wow, Landry, these are beautiful." She said as she tried them on, feeling like a princess. "Wow. They're so comfy. Thank you."

"There's something else in the box," Seo-Joon said, picking up the box and waiting for her to look at it.

"What is this?" She asked, picking up the envelope and then looking at them. "Are you spoiling me?"

"Totally," they said in unison.

"What?" Seo-Yeon said, staring at the voucher for a designer bridal shop. "What, what is this?"

"Landry said that I needed to play Fairy Godmother." Seo-Joon joked. "So, we got you an appointment at the store, so you can pick the wedding dress, and we'll pay for it."

"What? No, no, no, absolutely not."

"Yes, yes, absolutely yes," Landry said. "We want to do this for you. Let us."

"This is way too generous," Seo-Yeon said, frowning as she looked at Landry, then gave her a quick hug.

"You're welcome," Seo-Joon said before she hugged him tightly.

"I can't believe this, thank you, thank you. My shoes are beautiful. I need to buy a beautiful dress as well." She grinned at them before sitting next to Landry and staring at her shoes. Before she caught Landry's eye. They were pooling with tears, and Seo-Yeon couldn't help but take her hand in hers and squeeze it. This was probably Landry's way of saying goodbye before the inevitable storm engulfed them, and for that, Seo-Yeon was grateful. She would cherish this memory of the three of them forever.

Chapter eighteen

Lewis

Four weeks later, Australia

After breakfast, Lewis went back to the hotel room to change. Ever since they'd arrived in Sydney, he asked Seo-Yeon to pinch him just so he knew that he wasn't dreaming. Since living in Korea, Lewis learned to deal with his longing for his own country. It was often ignored. And a few times every month, he even dreamed about the warm waters and the beautiful sunsets of his childhood.

It was clear that all those years of self-imposed exile had never diminished his love for Australia. It'd just changed a bit because he'd learned to associate the country with the worst things that could have ever happened to a child. However, looking at the beach from his hotel room, all he wanted was to dive deep into the sea and let it welcome him back home.

His thoughts were interrupted by a knock on the door. He frowned, walking to it before finding Dr. Shim on the other side of the door. He stepped to the side and then let him walk in before closing the door.

"Morning." He said to Lewis and then looked around the room. "Are you ready?'

"Yes, I was just going to call a cab."

"I already have a driver downstairs." Dr. Shim told him as he clasped his hands together. "Shall we then?"

"Oh, I thought Seo-Yeon was coming with me," Lewis said in confusion as Dr. Shim smiled at him.

"She's going to go out with the ladies to do some shopping, and Seo-Joon and Landry will stay in their room because she's exhausted."

"Oh, okay. So you're escorting me?" He asked though he was sure this meant that Dr. Shim would be going with him to the prison where his father was. Lewis wanted to argue against this development, but he had a hunch that Dr. Shim, like Seo-Yeon, wouldn't let him dictate what he could or couldn't do. Defeated, Lewis took his wallet and smiled at him. "Shall we then?"

Dr. Shim nodded as he opened the door and walked out. Lewis made sure the door was closed before walking faster to catch up with Seo-Yeon and Seo-Joon's father. He was just a few inches shorter than Lewis, but his strides were longer, and Lewis had to almost jog to catch up.

He wasn't sure why Dr. Shim had decided to come with him, but he was grateful. It wasn't like he was very close to him. After all, Dr. Shim was always very busy with the hospital. The times they all had family dinners, though, he'd treated Lewis like a son. And he'd always been deeply appreciative about that. Especially after they found out that Lewis was dating Seo-Yeon. His biggest fear was that they would disapprove of their relationship because his family background was so different.

Dr. Shim didn't talk much. He'd been scrolling down his phone and answering emails on the way to the prison. Lewis felt a new desire to thank him but stopped himself. If Seo-Yeon had been there with him, she'd probably been talking non-stop, trying to help him relax.

However, this was precisely what he needed, and he wondered if that was the reason as to why Dr. Shim had come with him.

"Here we are." He finally said as the car pulled in front of the jail, and Lewis went to pay, but Dr. Shim beat him to it.

He climbed out of the car and then waited on his future father-in-law before leading the way to the front door, where they would have to go through security. Once inside, they were escorted to a room with a glass dividing it. They took a seat in front of the glass window and waited until Lewis's father walked into the room on the other side of the window.

Lewis's jaw clenched once his father sat in front of them.

"What the fuck are you doing here? Trying to keep me in jail still?" Lewis's father said before coughing,

Lewis cleared his throat before lifting his eyes to look at his father. His father had grown older, but his eyes' coldness had remained the same.

"I came to tell you that I forgive you."

His father gave him an incredulous look before he laughed. "Forgive me? Isn't that awful grand of you?" He coughed again then leaned closer to the window glass. "You have nothing to forgive me for. I did nothing but work and provide for you and that whore who was your mother."

Lewis's hand balled into a fist, but Dr. Shim placed his hand over it and stopped him from lunging at the glass. His father offered him a twisted smile, then nodded toward Dr. Shim.

"You brought a lawyer with you? You must be terrified." He said and then leaned back against the chair. "Your brothers will want a word with you."

"Well, they might, but they'll have to serve their time first in Korea," Lewis said and then shrugged. "Did you not know that Joshua and Peter were arrested for assaulting me and intimidating my fiancée."

"You put them in jail? You mother—"

"You know, I just wanted to say thank you." Dr. Shim said as Lewis' father turned to look at him, confused.

"Thank you? What the fuck for?"

"Well, you set the bar really low when it comes to Fathers, so I've been fortunate that you did that because that way Lewis thinks I'm an awesome father." Dr. Shim said, nodding. "You see, you fucked up." He said, standing up and buttoning his jacket. "You didn't know how precious your son was, and you chose violence. I know what a precious son he is. So, I'll only give him words of love and encouragement to change all the unkind words you sewed into his soul because he's *my* son. Has been for years now since he met my eldest during their military service. And soon, he'll legally belong to us. You see, in Korea, usually, a daughter gets removed from the register and added to her husband's family register." He explained. "But I love Lewis so much, he'll be added to mine. He'll be my son until his last day on this earth. And I'll make damn sure to show him what a real father is. So, thank you for the opportunity to become a better father." He said as he placed his hand on Lewis's shoulder. "Let's go, *son*." He said in Korean as he patted his shoulder gently and then opened the door for him and Lewis to walk out of the visiting area.

Lewis didn't know what to say, so he followed Dr. Shim in silence until they reached the front doors that led the way outside. When they stopped walking near a bench, Lewis held Dr. Shim's swear under his breath. Surprised, he turned and then smiled.

"That was pretty cool," Lewis told him.

"And I meant every word." Dr. Shim replied. "I do hope that you get closure now. We're your family, and we'll make sure that you're loved like you should have been loved as a child. We sometimes don't express it very well, but we all know we owe you a lot. Especially how you took care of Seo-Yeon when she couldn't talk to us or her brother. You always protected her, and there are no amount of words that I can use to express how grateful I am for you. There's no way I could ever repay your kindness and the love you have for her."

"Dr. Shim—"

"Abeojim, just call me Abeojim." He told him before patting his shoulder and looking around. "Shall we walk for a while? I feel like stretching my legs before going back to the hotel, plus Seo-Yeon and everyone else will be busy. We might as well find somewhere to have lunch, just us."

"I would love to," Lewis replied while they started to walk to the right, following the road as Lewis felt his eyes prickle.

It was the first time in all of his life that he really felt what it was like to have a father. And he was going to enjoy the way this moment felt until it was recorded entirely in his memory, so he could treasure it forever.

Chapter nineteen

Seo-Yeon

After breakfast the next day, Seo-Yeon led Lewis to the front of the hotel, where a cab was waiting for him. She gave the driver the address for Waverley Cemetery and then took Lewis's hand in hers after buckling up. When he gave her a quizzical look, she simply smiled at him.

"We don't have flowers," Lewis said, his forehead wrinkling with worry.

"Michael helped me sort that out. I ordered her favorites, and they were already delivered this morning." She said, squeezing his hand before linking their fingers together.

"Thank you," he said, meeting her eyes, and she could see the tears in his eyes.

This whole trip had been emotionally taxing on him, and she wanted to do something nice for him ahead of their wedding. She just hoped that today was a day when he could look back on the happy memories of his life with his mother rather than dwell on the way she was taken from him. Seo-Yeon looked out the window, saying a silent prayer for the skies to remain as blue as they were at that moment. She leaned her head back and sighed contently.

"The breeze is so gentle." She said, breaking the silence between them.

"Indeed, it's a nice day, not too hot, not too sticky." He said, bringing her knuckles to his lips. "I don't know what else you have prepared for today, but I have to say, thank you. Because I might forget afterward."

"Me? Nothing else." She shrugged with a knowing smile as she watched him. "Just trust me, today is going to be an amazing day," Seo-Yeon added as the cab finally pulled over outside the cemetery. Lewis paid the fare and then joined Seo-Yeon on the other side of the sidewalk. He looked around for a moment as he fixed his tie and then ran his hands through the bottom part of the jacket, as she'd seen him do countless times. It was an indication of how anxious he felt. She grabbed his clammy hand and then led the way inside, though he soon took the lead as he knew where he was going. Seo-Yeon looked at the different gravestones, which seemed extremely old before Lewis stopped.

"Did you forget where we're going?"

"No," he replied and then pointed toward the left side of the cemetery in the distance. "My godparents are buried somewhere in that area." He explained once he started to walk again. "Mom's buried with my grandparents with a view of the ocean. It was good that she had some savings and that she'd paid half of the burial with the money that my grandparents had left her." He added before he led her down the side of the road to an area that looked slightly newer than the previous one, but the headstones still looked quite weathered.

"It's nice that she's with her parents," Seo-Yeon said, thinking of her grandparents who were buried in a plot in Yongin Catholic Park Cemetery. Her mother's twin sister was buried with them.

"Yeah, she's not alone," Lewis said, clenching his jaw before stopping.

Seo-Yeon placed her hand on his lower back and leaned her head against his shoulder. "I can see the flowers." She said, knowing he probably would need a few minutes. At that moment, she felt eternally grateful for Michael. He'd taken a photo of the flowers as soon as they were placed on the grave. It was easy for her to take over now and lead the way to it.

"They're beautiful." He said, his voice breaking as he followed her. Lewis broke completely once they reached it, and Seo-Yeon knelt beside him on the ground, patting his back, hoping to reassure him.

"I never meant to fail her," Lewis whispered between sobs while Seo-Yeon felt the tears streaming down her cheeks. She reached in her bag for a packet of tissues handing him one.

"You never failed her," Seo-Yeon said firmly while she waited for him to take the tissue.

"I don't know about that," Lewis replied as she cupped his cheeks in her hands and then shook her head once more.

"You are here. You grew up well, got a job, served the military in a country that isn't your birth country, trained to be a chef, and got your diploma." She listed slowly as her eyes remained in his. "You became a good man who doesn't abuse others. I'm sure you're everything she wanted you to be and more, Lewis."

"Do you believe that?" He asked in a whisper, sounding like a child. Her heart hurt badly for him, and she did the only thing she knew would soothe his soul at that very moment. Seo-Yeon held him tight in her arms. "I believe that and more."

She looked at the headstone letting go of him. "Your mother was beautiful." She said, staring at the pictures framed next to the names. Her eyes were glued to a picture of Lewis and his mother, beaming at the camera on the beach.

"She was a babe when she had me." He explained and then leaned closer, touching the cold headstone. "She loved the ocean. So, we would go to the beach often. And that was her favorite picture of us." He pointed at the picture Seo-Yeon had been looking at and then nodded. "I would like to name one of our girls after her as a middle name."

"Of course," Seo-Yeon said, knowing that he would definitely keep that promise.

"But only as a middle name. Mildred is such an old woman's name." He joked as he gently let his fingers touch flower bouquets.

"It was your grandmother's name as well, right?" Seo-Yeon said.

"You just proved my point." He said and then laughed. "She also hated her name."

"I'm sure that our girl will love it," Seo-Yeon told him when he turned to look at him. "I do believe that'll be the case."

"Good luck writing it in Korean." He added as she laughed this time, holding on to his arm.

"We'll figure it out." She promised before he took her hand in his and then lifted it.

"See, Mom, I did manage to land a good one." He told the pictures before he kissed Seo-Yeon's hand.

Seo-Yeon wasn't sure how long they'd been in front of the family grave, but when Lewis suggested a walk, she followed him through the graveyard until they found a small boardwalk right on the shoreline. Lewis draped his arm around her waist while looking toward the ocean. The sun felt warm on her skin, making her feel slightly hotter than before, but she wasn't about to push him away. "Let's take a picture together." He requested after stopping in one of the corners and waiting for people to walk by. It was clear he didn't want any strangers in the background. Lewis held up his phone and then leaned closer to Seo-Yeon, kissing the top of her head as the ocean crashed against the rocks behind them. After taking a few pictures, he pocketed the phone, and just when Seo-Yeon was about to ask if he wanted to go back, his hands cupped her cheeks, and he kissed her deeply.

Seo-Yeon kissed him back, her heart full of love and lust. She pressed her body against his, letting her hands caress the nape of his neck. She was glad that she'd resisted being set up on countless blind dates, and instead, she'd waited for Lewis because he was her soulmate.

Chapter twenty,

Lewis

The following day, Lewis woke up to the sound of knocking. He sighed against the pillow, wondering why he'd bothered putting a do not disturb sign on the door. The truth was that he'd been expecting Seo-Yeon to stay with him. However, her mother asked her to go for a walk with her after dinner. And that'd been the last he'd seen of his fiancée. He still wondered how they would pull together the entire wedding because it seemed that there was no plan, and something deep inside of him was half happy about it.

One thing had definitely changed. New memories were rooting in his mind, getting rid of all the sad stuff. And he was definitely looking forward to his marriage to Seo-Yeon erasing the very last bitter memories he had. Being in Australia with Seo-Yeon, her parents, and their friends would undoubtedly change his feelings about Australia.

"I'm coming!" he said, aggravated as the knocks got louder and then stared at his friends when the door opened. "You fuckers."

"Hope you slept well," Seo-Joon said, pushing his way inside the room.

"What the hell are you doing here?" Lewis asked as he was about to close the door after Simon walked in, but Tae-Hyung pushed it open again. "You too? What are you all up to?"

"We're going surfing," Simon said enthusiastically. Lewis gave him and the others an are-you-out-of-your-ever-loving-minds look.

"What? Michael hooked us up with a sweet spot-on Bondi beach. He even texted, see?" Seo-Joon said, chuckling his phone at Lewis for him to see the text.

"Wait, it's five? Five in the morning? Are you guys kidding me?"

"Nope, here, go get ready," Tae-Hyung added as he handed him a bag.

"I hate you. I fucking hate you lot." He said, walking to the bathroom still cursing before he got in the shower.

Lewis walked out of the bathroom fifteen minutes later to find them by the door. He left the towel in the rack to dry, fixing his suspicious eyes on them

"Come on, dude," Simon said in the worst mix of American and Australian accents he'd ever heard before Lewis joined them.

"Don't do that ever again. That's the worst Australian accent in the history of the world."

"Whatever." Simon sulked as he followed Tae-Hyung and Seo-Joon into the elevator.

"Who's driving?" Lewis asked, thinking he didn't want to die before his wedding, and he was sure that as much as his friends tried to do good things, sometimes they backfired.

"We hired a driver." Seo-Joon chimed in as the doors closed.

"Cool," Lewis replied, thinking that was rather weird. "You know I lived here. I could have driven there."

"It's too early," Simon said as the doors opened and Dr. Shim walked in the elevator holding several coffee cups in a box.

"Good morning. Wow, you're up early." He said, offering the coffee cups to them.

"Why are you up, Abeojim? Don't you want to have a lie-in, so you can rest a bit before we go back to Seoul?" Lewis asked, taking one of the coffee cups.

"I'm fine. I felt like going for a walk, but then I thought maybe I should join you since Seo-Joon said you would go surfing."

"Do you surf, sir?" Tae-Hyung asked as Dr. Shim nodded.

"Appa even won a few trophies when we lived in Hawaii," Seo-Joon explained as the doors opened again in the lobby.

"Really?" Tae-Hyung said, impressed by Dr. Shim's apparent surfing skills. "That's really awesome. I have an extra bodysuit. It should fit you."

"Oh, well, let me tell the Missus." Dr. Shim said as they spilled out of the elevator, and Lewis frowned.

"What's wrong?" Seo-Joon asked as Lewis looked around.

"I smell bullshit, but I don't know what kind of bullshit," Lewis replied, suspiciously glancing at his friends.

"I've no idea what you're talking about," Seo-Joon smirked as he walked through the open front door.

Lewis grew even warier as he drank his coffee and noticed that they'd driven the short distance to Bondi Beach. He frowned once the van pulled over, and Seo-Joon and Simon rushed to its back to grab a few big pieces of luggage.

"Where are the boards?" Lewis asked, chucking his empty cup in a recycling bin near him, and then turned to look at his friends.

"Michael said he would take care of everything. Let's go change." Seo-Joon said as Tae-Hyung and Dr. Shim walked ahead with Simon.

Lewis followed them to the amenities to change into their wetsuits, but he noticed that they kept walking. Then, Simon ducked into an improvised tent. A frown settled on his face before stepping inside the tent.

"Surprise!" Simon and the others yelled as Lewis looked around, confused.

There were two full-length mirrors and tuxes on hangers in a near rack.

"What the hell?"

"Michael helped Seo-Yeon organize the wedding." Dr. Shim said with a smile. "I'm sorry that we've deceived you, son." He said, patting his shoulder.

Lewis blinked a few times. Seo-Yeon had told him that she would take care of everything, but he wondered if she'd gotten cold feet as the days had gone by. The fact that she didn't mention the wedding and that he'd gone to see his father had Lewis slightly worried, but he'd tried not to think about it too much.

"Wedding? It's not even half-past six."

"She wants to say her vows as the sun rises," Seo-Joon said with a grin. "My sister is nothing but a romantic."

"I can't believe you all were in on this."

"Believe it, now get dressed," Tae-Hyung said as he pointed at a corner where all his clothes were laid out.

"I have no idea how to … what to say even." He said, turning toward them.

"Well, I would say thank you, but Seo-Yeon actually did all the work with the girls. And Michael." Seo-Joon told him.

"Maybe just thank us for not letting you sleep in," Simon added, and Lewis bit his lip.

"Thank you then." He said, walking to the place where the clothes were, wondering how he'd gotten so lucky.

Lewis and his friends and father-in-law walked out of the tents ten minutes later and strolled across the beach to the small area set for the wedding. A small archway made out of reclaimed driftwood and adorned by countless wildflowers. Not far from that, there was a small table with a book, and two pens, which he guessed were for them to sign after marriage. A few chairs were strewn around, and as he looked toward the beach, he noticed the immensity of the blue ocean.

For a moment, Lewis could have sworn he'd seen his mother rushing toward the water, and diving in, loving it almost as much as a fish did. A smile settled on his lip as he noticed Michael walking over to stand with his friends.

"You traitor," Lewis told Michael as he gave Michael a hug.

"Sorry, Seo-Yeon made me promise I wouldn't tell you after Seo-Joon put me in contact with her," Michael explained, giving him another quick hug.

"I missed you," Lewis said.

"Me too, brother, me too." He said, looking around. "You're not going to regret this. Seo-Yeon looks so beautiful." He told him as Lewis shook his head.

"Hey, that's Mrs. Parker to you, and you better not say she looks beautiful again. I shouldn't want to kill you on my wedding day." He joked. "We better get into position." He said since he couldn't get married without Michael by his side.

"Treat me nicely; I'm about to perform your wedding," Michael replied with a grin before taking his place behind Lewis and his friends as the music started.

The girls walked together, Landry, Lorena, and Sarah, before Seo-Yeon's parents walked down the aisle with her.

Lewis felt as if he'd been kicked in the chest when he saw her. His eyes welling, he wanted to run to her. It took all of his willpower not to leave his spot. Seo-Yeon looked beautiful, and he knew then what he'd known all along. He would love her till his dying breath.

Chapter twenty-one

Seo-Yeon

The breezy beach was deserted, just like Michael had promised, and as Seo-Yeon walked with her parents down the aisle, she took everything in. The wedding arch had been carefully covered in wildflowers, and so had the small table where they would sign their marriage certificate. The few chairs they needed were covered in white fabric with tulle and bows in the back that held together even more flowers.

Her mother said it best when they arrived on the beach a few hours earlier. This would be the tiniest but most beautiful wedding. And Seo-Yeon agreed wholeheartedly. She'd never wanted a big wedding, even when Seo-Joon had insisted on throwing a massive wedding for her and Lewis. She wanted this. All the people who mattered the most to her. Her parents, her brother, Landry, her friends, and Lewis.

After handing the flower bouquet to Landry, she took Lewis's hands in hers and squeezed them tight. She beamed at him and then bit her bottom lip when it started to tremble. Her make-up wouldn't survive the blubber fest if she began to cry.

"You're so beautiful." He said, sobbing softly as Michael cleared his throat behind them.

"Good morning, everyone." Michael started in his Australian twang before reading a few verses from the bible and then looked at Lewis and Seo-Yeon. "Friends, and Family, we're all gathered today to witness love. Or as Seo-Joon suggested, what nagging and wearing someone down can get you." He said as everyone laughed, and no one laughed the loudest other than Seo-Joon. "Lewis said he got lucky when he met Seo-Yeon, but he learned what true, self-less love meant when she agreed to marry him, despite his circumstances. And Seo-Yeon said she couldn't agree more." He added as everyone laughed again. "I've known Lewis since the womb, as our mothers were pregnant simultaneously. I have to say that after meeting Seo-Yeon and spending time with her yesterday, I can see why he fell so totally in love with her. But can't help noticing that she's marrying well beneath her."

"Oi, stop that." Lewis joked as he dried the tears with his handkerchief.

"Let's wrap this up before the groom floods the beach." He said with a wink as Lewis sighed.

After putting away the handkerchief, Lewis retook her hands and lifted them to his lips, kissing them gently. "Seo-Yeon," he started. "I still remember that stormy day when I first met you. Seo-Joon had invited me over to dinner because it was our first leave, and I had no one to spend it with. And then Simon tagged along because he's annoying like that." He said, glancing at Simon quickly before he looked at her again. "You were so young and so independent. But most of all, you were so compassionate." He told her as she could see him trying to control his emotions. "You were beautiful, but you were also Seo-Joon's sister, and I was afraid that I would ruin our friendship if I asked you out. But I didn't really have anything to worry about since you refused to date me." He said as Seo-Yeon laughed and the rest of the guests. "You made me wait because you knew that I had to sort through things and grow up. Even though I was older than all of you, I was still stuck in the past in many ways. You gave me strength even when you were breaking my lustful heart." He told her, lifting his hand to her cheek. "I was so totally in love with you back then, and now, it feels as if that love has grown so much stronger. I can't wait to walk the rest of our lives together. Together, we'll follow the cherry blossoms' path in the spring and go fishing in the summer. And we'll adopt a bunch of rugrats who are ours, but God had to, so kindly, send them to us through other parents." He added before he kissed her cheek. "I love you."

Seo-Yeon grinned at him, mouthing I love you before she controlled her emotions enough to speak.

"I never knew that I would love someone as much as I love my family." She began and then felt her body shaking. "Meeting you, falling in love with you, trusting you, after everything that happened in my life strengthened my faith in people. I thank God for putting you in the same unit as Seo-Joon." She said with a slight chuckle. "I've never been so loved, so cherished, and I've never loved or cherished anyone as much I cherish you." She nodded. "I can't wait to go into the world together to find those babies as a married couple." She bit her lip as her eyes welled. "And I can only pray that we have many years together. So, we can love each other and our future family to the fullest. I love you." She said as Michael gave her a tissue.

"Friends, Family, we're witnessing a new family born today." He said as Lewis slid the ring on her finger, and Seo-Yeon did the same.

"By the power invested in me by the Waverly Council, I pronounce you Husband and Wife." He said, offering them the warmest of smiles. "You may kiss the bride."

Lewis pulled Seo-Yeon closer, dipping her gently before his lips closed over hers, as she held on tightly to him and kissed him. Lewis pulled her up gently when the kiss was over and draped an arm around her. They took a few steps to the right, where her parents were for a deep bow. She knew her mother had had her heart set on a traditional wedding. One with the bride wearing a hanbok; however, Seo-Yeon had preferred the off-shoulder dress with the flowing skirt. It was too warm, after all, for the hanbok. Still, she promised her mother that once they were back in Korea, she would organize a reception for the rest of the family and friends and wear a hanbok of her choosing.

Seo-Yeon's parents stood up and held them tight in their arms for a moment before her mother sighed.

"I can't believe all our kids are settled now." She looked at Seo-Yeon and then Lewis before glancing at Seo-Joon and Landry. "I'm so happy today." She added with a slight nod before Dr. Shim congratulated them.

Seo-Yeon and Lewis took the center of the improvised stage. Slightly confused, they looked at the chairs, standing there while Lorena swiped something on the phone. A few seconds later, it registered that Simon and Tae-Hyung were singing one of her favorite songs. It was an original Talisman song and one of the first ballads that won them awards at the Music Shows in Korea before helping them raise their international profile.

Lewis took her hand in his before his arm draped around her waist and pulled her closer, swaying gently to the song. "Happy?"

"The happiest." She agreed with a smile before he leaned closer and kissed her. Seo-Yeon felt as if she were riding on the wings of doves, flying high above the world, somewhere where sadness didn't exist. Her only hope then was for their marriage to be just as exhilarating and sweet as their wedding had been.

Chapter twenty-two,
Lewis

After returning from Australia, Sung-Rok had paid them a visit at home. He'd brought wine and Seo-Yeon's favorite ice-cream cake. Lewis sighed, still feeling annoyed because Sung-Rok had been trying to lessen the blow. While he and Seo-Yeon had been in Australia, his brothers had managed to get themselves extradited, escaping the eight years sentence in South Korea.

Sung-Rok apologized profusely for having to tell them about it, but he wanted Seo-Yeon and Lewis to know the truth.

Lewis remembered then how he wanted that to be the end of the story, but days later, a call from Michael made things worse. Neither of his brothers had lasted long in jail. Michael believed that they'd stepped on toes that they shouldn't have, and now an all-out war had broken between them and new drug dealers in the area. After the last call ten days ago, Lewis figured that Peter and Joshua were buried. And most probably, their father was once more in charge of everything.

He left the office and walked back to the restaurant surveying the operation. The new waiter kept messing up, even though Lewis'd taken time off to train himself. He watched the boy walk back to the kitchen, ensuring he wouldn't drop the tray, and Lewis couldn't help but breathe out, relieved.

He returned to the maître d' station to check the bookings. Christmas was really starting to pick up, and more and more people were making reservations to hold parties and receptions at the restaurant. At first, only Kpop fans were making bookings in the hopes of seeing their favorites. Soon, they started getting accolades and great reviews by Korean insiders and foodies worldwide. Lewis knew that part of the initial success was due to Talisman having often been seen at the restaurant. The rest was due to Landry and Seo-Yeon's hard work creating a buzz on the different Social Media platforms.

"How's it going?" Seo-Yeon asked as she walked toward him, waving at a few regular customers sitting not far from them.

"Booked solidly for the next week. And our party room is also booked until March." He told her with a smile before kissing her cheek.

"Stop." Seo-Yeon hissed as she looked around. "You don't want to put people off their food." She said and then cleared her throat. "You can always meet me in the office. There are a few things I would like to show you." She smirked as she turned around and walked toward the back of the restaurant.

Lewis shook his head, thinking she would be his death. He stayed rooted to the spot, looking over a few of the receipts, biding his time, before he walked back to the office and locked the door behind him.

"You *do* know everyone knows what we do here, right?" He asked as she unzipped her dress and shrugged.

"We're married."

"There's also a full restaurant." He said with a groan as she kissed him, pressing her body against him.

"And this way, we'll never stop being sexy and having hot sex," Seo-Yeon said before her hand slid down between them and unzipped his trousers.

"I should be in the kitchen."

"And yet, you followed me." She smirked against his lips.

He pulled her up in his arms and settled her on the tiny couch opposite the desk. "Are you really complaining?"

"Of course not, just stating the obvious." She said, lifting her hips so he could take off her panties.

"One of these days, we should have boring sex like married people are meant to do." He said, crushing his lips against hers as she raked her fingernails down his back. "Ow."

"Never boring." She said with a toothy grin before he bit the skin of her neck, and she let out a soft moan.

"I promise it'll never be boring." He agreed as he pulled her hips closer to him, as he felt his whole body fusing with hers, before returning his lips to hers.

Lewis let his hands caress her skin, moving slowly against her. He slowly kissed her neck as Seo-Yeon's legs tightened around his waist.

"Sir!" a knock on the door froze Lewis in place as he tried to remember if he'd locked the door or not. He glanced at it and sighed, relieved when he saw the door was indeed locked.

"There's a long-distance call for you, sir." The voice said again as Lewis shook his head.

"I should kill them." He whispered as Seo-Yeon giggled against his skin. "Please take a message!"

"I tried that, sir, but a man named Michael said he has to talk to you."

"Better yet, let's kill Michael," Lewis said, pulling away from her as Seo-Yeon groaned.

"I patched it through—"

"Yes, yes, whatever, I got it, thanks, Lucas." He said loudly and then shook his head as he punched the blinking light on the phone and then sighed. "Yes, Michael?"

"Sorry to call when you're in the middle of service, but I have news," Michael replied.

"What's wrong?"

"I don't know how to say this, but they're gone." He said after a pause, and Lewis frowned.

"What? Who's gone?"

"They— Your brothers and sisters, your dad."

"They left Australia? Was there another warrant for their arrest? Do you know where they went?" Lewis asked fast as he leaned against the desk.

"No, Lewis," Michael said softly. "The other drug-dealing family, they didn't just stop at killing Peter and Joshua in jail." He began as Lewis felt his stomach turn. "I got a call from the cops, there was an anonymous tip, and when the cops got there, they—" Michael stopped for a moment and then took a deep breath in and let it out.

"They were executed."

"What about the children?"

"Child protection has them."

"Were they all unharmed?"

"Your eldest nephew, Lance, he made sure to get the little ones out as soon as he saw the men. All six of them are safe."

Lewis nodded and then sighed. "Okay, that's good that the kids were not harmed." He said, feeling contrived because he couldn't tell if he was sad or happy even though the news shocked his system. He felt numb.

"I was asked by one of the detectives to identify the bodies, so I'll call you tomorrow once all of that is done."

"Sure, I'm sorry you have to deal with this in my stead."

"It's fine. I just wanted you to know."

Lewis hesitated for a moment and then spoke again. "What about the kids?" He frowned as Seo-Yeon moved closer, arching an eyebrow. "What do you mean?"

"Where will they go?"

"They were put with a foster family who had a vacancy for all six. And they had cribs for the babies. But that's just an emergency placement, and the court will review this by next week. They'll probably go in the system."

"No, that can't happen," Lewis said, shaking his head. "Those kids, my siblings were all mother fuckers, but those kids were not being brought up that way. They won't be brought up thinking that they're not loved or cherished," Lewis said firmly.

"What are you trying to say? Are you going to take care of them?"

"I have to talk to Seo-Yeon. Just make sure that they don't go into the system." He said, hanging up the phone turning to look at her. "What happened to the kids? Your siblings?"

"My family was taken out by a rival family." He said as she frowned.

"And the babies?"

"We're going to adopt those kids."

"Lewis, what if they don't want us?" Seo-Yeon asked, ever the practical woman, and Lewis smiled.

"They're all small kids. The oldest is Lance, and he's barely seven. He pulled all his cousins out of the house to safety. If that's not a Seo-Yeon in the making, I don't know what is."

She stared at him and then shook her head. "You'll have to explain why you didn't have contact with them until now. Why you didn't have contact with your family." She said, looking right in his eyes.

"I don't want those kids to grow up like I did. I don't want them to think they're not worthy of someone's affection. Or that they caused their parents' deaths." He told her as Seo-Yeon cupped his cheeks in her hands and nodded slowly.

"Okay, let's do it," Seo-Yeon said simply as he watched her, surprised. "I love you. Of course, I will jump off this cliff with you and hope our parachutes work."

"What parachutes?" he asked with a half-smile before kissing her. This was the most significant decision of their lives, and they'd made it in a few seconds. Somehow it all made sense. He thought as he pulled her to the sofa with him.

"Let's finish what we started."

Chapter twenty-three

Seo-Yeon

Seo-Yeon had driven with Sarah and Lorena outside of Seoul to Seo-Joon and Landry's house in the countryside. The house sat alone after a bridge and looked slightly out of place since most homes had a traditional style. Seo-Joon's house was more modern and western-looking, with an ample deck at the back that opened into the garden. After parking right outside the house, Lorena pressed the doorbell and stood near her studying her.

"What's wrong?" Lorena asked as they waited for the gate to open.

"I'll tell you inside." She promised as the buzzard rang loudly and the gate opened.

"How long are you staying here?" Seo-Yeon asked Sarah to try and shift the focus from her.

"I leave the day after tomorrow," Sarah told her as Lorena frowned.

"I thought you said you would stay one more week."

"Yes, but Gracie wants me back. She's ready to pop, and I need to be there to take over." Sarah pouted as Lorena patted her head.

"It'll be all right."

"I'll be back before the baby's born," Sarah replied. "Gracie's not taking a lot of maternity leave. I don't think she trusts me that much."

"Of course, she does. Otherwise, she wouldn't have hired you, Miss President." Seo-Yeon told her once they went up the stairs and the door opened.

"Hey, ladies."

"Doctor Shim, are you playing hooky?" Seo-Yeon asked her brother, and he shook his head.

"Of course not. I have a night shift today." He replied and then said hello to Lorena and Sarah.

"Oh, likely story," Seo-Yeon added as she walked in and kicked her shoes off before putting on one of the disposable slippers that Seo-Joon had left for them to wear.

"You ladies hungry? I was just preparing a fish soup for Landry, but I also have tteokbokki if you want to eat something else."

"Nah, we're fine. We had a late lunch before driving here." Seo-Yeon told him as she walked to the living room decorated in charcoal grey and white.

Landry managed to give it a minimalist touch, much to Seo-Joon's chagrin. He liked clutter, but she'd managed to get him to throw most of the old stuff out or donate it.

"Hey," Landry waved at them from the sofa as she scooted down and then leaned against the armrest to pull herself slightly straighter.

"Don't move. We're fine." Lorena said, giving her a tight hug before Seo-Yeon followed and finally Sarah.

Even though Sarah was Simon's twin, she was the one who recoiled from hugs the most. On the other hand, her brother had adopted American style manners when showing warmth and loved to hug people. Something that he refrained from doing a lot with fans, as some of them thought it was weird, and he almost got called a pervert once.

Seo-Yeon shook her head slightly so she wouldn't laugh at her recollections, knowing that Lorena would press for information.

"Oh, we did bring you some of your favorites.' Lorena said as she held up the cooler. "We stopped for bingsu." She announced as Landry nodded.

"You girls don't have to bring me food every time you see me. But is it melon bingsu?" She asked, referring to the delicious, shaved ice with condensed milk and generous scoops of honeydew melon.

"Of course," Seo-Yeon said.

"And beans?"

"Totally," Seo-Yeon replied, taking the cooler and walking to the kitchen so she could get some serving bowls.

"Here, I can give you these?" Seo-Joon said as Seo-Yeon frowned. "You've lost so much weight."

"I'm fine." Seo-Joon stirred the soup, then grabbed the big ladle and scooped most of the broth out before pouring it into a bowl.

"Mom and Dad are worried that you're not eating well or resting enough."

"I'm fine." Seo-Joon's voice was loud and cutting as Seo-Yeon watched him. "I'm sorry, I just—" he shrugged, defeated before he placed the bowl and the ladle on the counter and sighed, gripping it tightly.

"Let's go for a walk outside."

"No, I have to give this to Landry."

"I'll do it, Oppa," Sarah said, walking into the kitchen and looking between them. Seo-Yeon offered her a grateful smile.

"Come with me," Seo-Yeon said, taking his hand in hers like when they were children. They walked on the tiny path that led to the garden.

Roxette barked before running toward them and charged at Seo-Yeon, trying to give her a sloppy kiss. Seo-Yeon smiled at the dog and squatted for a few minutes beside her as she patted her head.

"I know this might be the most painful and difficult thing of your life." She began.

"I don't want to listen to this now, Seo-Yeon, please."

"You have to, Oppa." She said softly as she looked at him. "I love you more than anything. Mom and Dad know that." She told him with a smile. "Which is why I have to tell you this."

"I can't rest or do anything when I know she—"

"I know." She said, simply standing up and taking his hand in hers. "Any moment… All moments are precious right now. We're living on borrowed time."

"You still need to take care of yourself," Seo-Yeon told him.

"I'm not strong enough to do this." He said after a pause as tears streamed down his cheeks, and he bent over his knees. His hands held up the top part of his body as his head faced the floor under him.

Seo-Yeon moved closer, patting his back, as Roxette tried to comfort him, licking his hands.

"It's fine, I'm fine," Seo-Joon told the dog before she sat beside him.

"It's okay, girl." He said softly as he ran a hand through her fur.

"She can also smell your bullshit," Seo-Yeon told him as he looked up, shocked.

"Hey, I'm still your older brother, don't talk to me like that." He said in a stern tone before he pulled her into a hug. "Thank you, Seo-Yeon."

"Anything for my best friend and brother." She told him, patting his back.

"I'll try."

"I know you're just saying that not to worry me, so I'll take it." She said to him as Seo-Joon chuckled.

"Yes," he admitted and then kissed the top of her head. "Come on, I need to make sure Landry's comfortable before working."

"Is Eomma coming over tonight?"

"Can't keep her away even if I wanted to." He replied as they walked back to the house.

"It's nice, right?"

"What is?"

"Eomma and Appa are parents to Landry and Lewis." She said, nodding. "They were starved for parental love, and now they're being smothered by it."

"Hopefully, you and Lewis turn out just like them and will smother all those twenty-two kids Lewis wants to adopt." He joked as she shook her head.

"No, not twenty-two, but we're going to start with six."

"What do you mean six?"

"Let's go back inside, so I can tell you all simultaneously." She grinned at him, leading him back to the house.

Chapter twenty-four

Lewis

After meeting with a government official to discuss adopting his nephews and nieces, Lewis visited a friend of his in-laws. The man was an officer who worked for the South Korea Immigration office. He would help him, and Seo-Yeon navigate all the paperwork they had to fill out to legally bring the kids over.

For the first time in his life, he regretted leaving Australia. He regretted not doing enough to keep the children safe. The kids needed to be with him and Seo-Yeon as soon as possible. While these thoughts ran through his head, he took a seat in the designated area. He ran his hands through his hair, hoping that the process wouldn't be too complex or lengthy.

A few minutes later, a woman called him, using his Korean name, Shim Si-Woo, which he'd started using after getting engaged to Seo-Yeon. The woman led him to the back of the offices through a long hallway before a western-looking man greeted him with a smile.

"Are you Australian?" Lewis said without thinking as the man shook his head.

"I'm actually English but have been here for thirty years, so I *do* have a Korean name." He replied as he pointed at the seat. "I'm afraid I don't have a lot of time, but I've gathered all the materials you'll need to read through and the list of things we'll need before making a decision."

"Right, so, how long does it take for all of this to process?"

"I can't really tell you, it can take a few months, or it can be a few years, depending on how the courts' workload is. After what happened to that baby—" he said, referring to a small child who'd died months previously after being adopted. "We have to be extremely careful with every case that we see, and we're striving to do the very best for the children."

"Of course," Lewis said, frowning as he looked at the folders and then picked them up.

"Also, I don't want to discourage you, but it might take some time for the Australian government to go through all their investigations. They'll want to know why you weren't in contact with the family, why you didn't go back to Sydney in so many years. They'll want to know your relationship to the parents, your father." His voice trailed off as Lewis nodded.

"Yes, I know that."

"It's going to be difficult due to the estrangement. I don't want to discourage you, but this might not go the way you want, Mr. Parker."

"I understand. I like that you're being direct." Lewis replied as there was a knock on the door.

"I'm afraid that's all the time I have today." The man said, standing up as Lewis nodded.

"Thank you, I do appreciate you seeing me on such short notice." He said before shaking his hand and then bowed before walking out of the office.

Lewis wandered around for a while before he found himself right in front of the monument to Yi Sun-Si and then sighed, looking at it. This whole idea of his was starting to feel like a battle. Seo-Yeon didn't need this, he told himself as he watched the tourists taking pictures. She wanted a family, and he was willing to make them wait even longer because he thought he should take care of his nephews and nieces.

Maybe it'd been a crazy idea. Lewis thought as he kept walking down the island in the middle of the road, leaving Yi Sun-Si's monument behind before stopping right in front of King Seo-Jong's one.

Lewis stopped in front of the large monument and sighed. "Bet you didn't have these problems. You just had to develop a whole writing system and new alphabet." He said ruefully as he stared at the statue of the king before he walked around the base and then ducked into the small museum under it.

After walking around aimlessly for a while, admiring the exhibits and old Korean artifacts, he came out to the other side of the museum. He stopped at the traffic lights, facing the impressive palace that Seo-Yeon loved visiting. Always in hanbok. A smile settled on his lips as he was about to take a picture, but his phone alerted him to the text message.

He opened the message chat and read.

Hyung, are you busy?

What's up, Simon? He texted then proceeded to take a picture of the palace.

So many dramas had been filmed in that place, he was sure that he should order a print of the palace for the restaurant. The k-drama lovers who often visited his restaurant hoping to catch a glimpse of Simon would probably love it.

Lewis frowned as Simon didn't reply but instead called him.

"What's up?" Lewis asked after accepting the call.

"Hyung, where are you?"

"I'm right outside your house, Chona." He said, using the word for majesty since Simon had just finished a drama where he played the king.

"Gyeongbokgung?" Simon asked as Lewis moved to the side, as a few tourists were gathering around.

"Yes, I had to go to the Embassy. Are you okay?"

"Yeah, I'm just waiting with Lorena at the court. They called us to let us know that there was a child we could adopt. Father Matteo met him about six months ago when his mother was hospitalized. So, he helped them find him a bed in one of the orphanages. We were told to come and meet him, and if everything goes great, we can adopt him."

"How old is he?"

"Four, close to five."

"Wow, congrats, Simon."

"It's all happened so quickly."

"Are you chickening out now?"

"No, never. I'm just excited but scared. What if he doesn't like us?"

"He's going to love you and Lorena. I'm sure." Lewis told him, trying to reassure you. "And if not, he might just love Lorena more than you."

"That's not funny, Hyung."

"No, you're right. It was a cheap shot, but I had fun with that." He added with a chuckle. "Do you want me to come over?"

"Do you mind?"

"Of course not. Just send me the address."

"Thanks, Hyung," Simon said before Lewis pocketed the phone and then crossed the road to the side of the palace.

A few people walked by dressed in Hanboks nearby the children laughed, running as they blew bubbles. Lewis stopped to look at them before receiving the notification, then stepped to the curb to hail a taxi.

His eyes remained on the kids for a moment, and he didn't notice the taxi until the driver started yelling at him to get in. He climbed in the front seat next to the man apologizing before giving the man the address. Maybe things would work out for him and Seo-Yeon just like they had for Simon and Lorena. After all, stranger things had happened, right?

Chapter twenty-five
Seo-Yeon

The restaurant was empty, and Seo-Yeon made sure for the billionth time that everything looked perfect. She paced back and forth until she heard the elevator's bell and then forced a smile on her features before she walked to open the door to greet her parents.

"What's wrong?" Doctor Shim asked as he walked inside, and then Seo-Yeon closed the door since they were technically closed.

"I have news." She said as she nodded to the table that she'd set with food and then pulled the lids on the kimchi stew and the ribs.

"And you're feeding us first?" he asked, frowning as her mother shook her head.

"She's probably nervous, and I've not eaten." She said as he pulled out a chair for her to sit down, then Seo-Yeon's.

"What's wrong?" Doctor Shim asked as his wife turned to look at him.

"You're really dense sometimes, Yeobo." She said, and Seo-Yeon knew that even though her mother had called him Honey, it wasn't meant as a term of endearment.

Her parents hardly ever argued. Her father was controlled in his responses. The few times they'd had arguments, what had freaked her and Seo-Joon the most was that her mother never went into hysterics. She instead chose a low register of her voice and a smile on her face that was far scarier than anything else that she'd ever seen in a horror movie.

"It's obvious that something is wrong. I'm not dense." He blinked and then adjusted his tie before clenching his jaw.

"Okay, I'll tell you," Seo-Yeon said, knowing that they would not speak at this pace. "You know how we told you about what happened to Lewis's family in Australia."

"Yes, they were killed."

"Yes…" Seo-Yeon nodded. "And his nephews and nieces were taken away to be fostered."

"Wait, I thought the family would take them in." her mother said, and she could see the wheels turning in her head before Seo-Yeon spoke again.

"There's no one. The only relative that Michael found said that the mother had been dead a long time and the parents don't want to meet the grandchildren."

"What?" Doctor Shim hissed and then leaned back in the chair.

"That's terrible. Whatever problems they might have had with the mother, the children aren't to blame."

"That's why Lewis and I decided to apply to have sole custody of the children and adopt them." She said as fast as she could. They say ripping a plaster quickly causes less pain, and it should make this conversation go faster.

"What now?" her mother asked though Seo-Yeon knew that it wasn't a question because she'd not understood. She was asking to give Seo-Yeon a chance to explain the whole thing again and add more information.

"Lewis doesn't want them to go in the system when we can take them."

"But you live here." Her father said.

"Yes, we would bring them over."

"But then, you would have to move out of Lewis's apartment and buy a house, and it's not even sure that they'll give you the children. He's not had contact with them in years. Do they know him?" Her father asked as her mother remained awfully quiet.

"We know that too." She said and then clasped her hands tightly under the table. "Michael has handed our dossier, with all our paperwork, bank information, and pictures of a house that we saw, not far from Seo-Joon and Landry."

"But you haven't bought the house." Her father interjected as she looked at her mother, but she was quietly eating.

"No, but we've put in an offer."

"An offer, but you don't know how long this will go on for or how much money you'll have to spend."

"Appa," she said so he would stop freaking out. "These kids, they're babies. The eldest is seven, and he managed to get out five kids ranging from one-month-old to four." Seo-Yeon said, looking at him. "He heard the gunshots, and he knew. He knew what was going to happen. We can only imagine the kind of things he's endured, or the things he saw, to know what was going to happen if he didn't take himself and his cousins out of the house." She said, looking at him.

"And you'll have to find a therapist for him."

"So what?" She asked softly, looking at him.

"Jin-Ah, say something." He said to his wife as she shrugged.

"What do you want me to say? These children need help."

"You can't possibly support their decision to get into this mess. They just got married." Doctor Shim said, looking at his wife horrified.

"What do you want me to say, Sung-Joon?" She asked, placing the chopsticks down and then turning completely to look at him. "First, you asked me why I was allowing Seo-Joona to marry a woman who was dying, and now this? When have I ever stopped them from doing what they wanted?"

"Jin-Ah…" he groaned, looking at her. "This is different."

"No, it's not. It's exactly what your parents tried to do when you introduced me to them." She said, watching him. "They asked who my parents were and then tried to make you break up with me because I was raised by an unmarried aunt who took my brother and me in after mother and father died." She said, shaking her head. "If they want to do what my Immo did for my brother and me, I'm not going to stop them." She said, referring to her aunt, picking up the chopsticks before picking one of the ribs up and putting it on her plate.

"That's very unfair." Doctor shim replied as Seo-Yeon smiled at her mother.

"Your parents were snobs," Seo-Yeon said, and then her mother laughed.

"You don't know the half of it, but now they adore me." She said, elbowing her husband. "Give your blessing and help me pray for them and the children when we go to church tonight."

He sighed and shook his head. "Of course," he began and then took Seo-Yeon's hand in his. "Just don't go into this blindly. You'll have to find therapists and make sure that the children don't bear a lot of traumas from this."

"Of course, Appa. And Lewis is already looking for doctors with Seo-Joon and everything we need. And when the call comes, you'll be the first to know. Lewis promised he'll call you both so you know when your grandchildren will get here."

"No, no, don't say that. You'll jinx yourselves." He said, squeezing her hand before letting go of it. "Just don't get ahead of yourselves. You just got married, and you still don't have a house. What if they turn you down?"

"Sung-Joon, stop being so negative." Her mother said and then put one of the ribs on his plate on top of the rice. "Just eat, it's good, it'll make you happy, and you'll stop talking nonsense." She added as he scowled at her for a moment before he had some of the meat.

"Thank you, Eomma… Appa." Seo-Yeon said, nodding before she tucked in her food as well.

Chapter twenty-six

Lewis

After getting a few water bottles, he met Lorena and Simon in the Ministry of Health and Wellness lobby and followed them into the elevator. He could tell how freaked out they both were and decided not to crack any jokes. He was sure that Lorena would stab him with the file in her hand, and Simon would probably hyperventilate badly. Once they stepped out of the elevator, they walked down the long corridor as an older woman greeted them. Lewis took a step back, giving them some space as she opened the door into a room where he could see a tiny little boy.

He watched them going in, feeling as if he should stop intruding in their moment, but he wanted to see how it would all go. After all, Simon and Lorena longed for a child almost immediately after getting engaged. It was a miracle that she'd gotten pregnant at all, and then this. Another miracle where they were able to adopt a child. Lewis turned his back to the door and looked out the window behind him, wondering if he would be able to make that dream for him and Seo-Yeon a reality. He'd never thought much about having children until he'd fallen for Seo-Yeon. Then all he could think about was being with her forever and having their own family. He picked up his phone, opened the messaging app, and smiled at her profile picture.

Simon and Lorena are getting their boy today. I'm with them now, so I'll message you once I leave.

He twisted the bottle's cap before taking a swig and then looked at the text message's reply.

It's good you're there. I'm going over the receipts at the restaurant. If you want a lift, just come back to the restaurant, and we can go home together.

Lewis sent her a winking face before he heard the door opening behind him. The woman smiled at him, bowing slightly.

"Are you friends?" She asked in English before Lewis nodded.

"Yes, we are. Been friends for a long time since we served together in the military." He replied in Korean as she looked at him, surprised before she laughed.

"Oh wow, you speak Korean." She said, nodding.

"I try." Lewis joked as she shook her head at him.

"Well, I think Jun-Myeon wants to go home with them. But we're going to give them thirty minutes to be acquainted first. If you want to say hello, you can go in." She explained.

"No, it's fine. I'll wait here so he doesn't get freaked out by the weird Western-looking guy." He said as she nodded with a smile and then walked away, leaving him alone in the hallway.

By the time Simon and Lorena came out of the room with Jun-Myeon, the little boy looked a lot at ease with Lorena, holding on to her hand. Lewis watched him closely and then smiled when Simon crouched beside him.

"This is my friend, Lewis. You can call him uncle." Simon told him as the little boy moved behind Lorena without letting go of her hand.

"It's fine. You can say hello another day." He told the boy as Simon straightened and then grinned at him.

"Isn't he cute?" Simon asked as Lewis nodded.

"I know you're totally going to lose your wife to him." Lewis teased him as Lorena smacked his arm playfully but still hard enough. Lewis knew that she was going to leave a mark.

"We're going to go now, but thank you for coming over," Lorena told Lewis as Simon picked Jun-Myeon up after explaining that Lorena couldn't pick him up.

"It's my pleasure." He told them as they all bundled up in the elevator. "Simon." He said as Simon looked like he was about to hyperventilate. "You're going to do fine." He told him as Simon thanked him.

"Do you really think so?"

"Out of you, Seo-Joon and me, you're the dad." He nodded. "You're going to do fine."

"God willing," Simon replied as they exited the elevator. Then Lewis said his goodbyes in the lobby after Dae-Jung and David, Simon's manager and Lorena's bodyguard, joined them.

Lewis watched them for a moment, walking to the other side of the building, probably because they had a car waiting there, to take them back home without the press finding out.

He walked out of the building and then sighed, closing his eyes slightly as the warm breeze touched his skin. Rather than walking and taking the metro, he hailed a taxi, deciding that it would be better to get back to Seo-Yeon as fast as he could.

Half an hour later, Lewis took the elevator inside the Lotte World Tower and got out on the restaurant's floor. The place was packed with the evening crowd. The new waitressing staff and the manager worked in unity as if they'd been doing that for years. He nodded at the manager and then walked behind the maître d' counter to check on the evening takings before going back to the office.

"Hey, beautiful." He said, locking the door behind him.

Seo-Yeon arched an eyebrow watching him intently.

"You're buttering me up?" Seo-Yeon asked before her eyes narrowed playfully. "What did you do?"

"Nothing, but we should enjoy the kinky sex before getting the kids." He said as she returned her eyes to the monitor before lifting the cup of tea to her lips.

"Maybe."

"Maybe?" Lewis asked, frowning as he leaned over her shoulder to look at the monitor. "Yikes, is that last week's money?"

"Yes," Seo-Yeon kissed his cheek.

"It's not that bad." He sighed, straightening up, and then ran a hand through his hair and face.

"I also got a call from the estate agent."

"And?"

"He said we were approved." She said before he pulled her chair back away from the desk and then pulled her into his arms, kissing her tenderly.

"I knew it was going to be good news."

"Well, hold your horses. That doesn't mean we have the house."

"No, but we're approved, so we can get something like it even if it's not that one. I'm fine with that."

"And Michael called. He said he had news, but he'll call in the morning."

"Okay." He said, settling her on her feet.

"And I told my parents."

"You did?" Lewis couldn't help but grin. "How upset were they?"

"Not upset, just concerned." She said after thinking about the word for a moment. "Eomma actually Sung-Joon, my dad."

"And I missed that?" He sulked. "That's so unfair."

"So, how's Lorena and Simon's baby?"

"He's so cute. He actually looks a lot like Simon, and funnily enough, Lorena." He nodded. "I mean, I don't think anyone could tell he's adopted."

"Well, they'll tell him eventually." She said, biting her bottom lip.

"What's wrong?"

"I just hope it happens for us too." She said as he pulled her closer and kissed her neck.

"It will. I have a really good gut feeling about this all. Trust me." He said before kissing her tenderly, as he hoped that Michael had good news for them.

Chapter twenty-seven

Seo-Yeon

Michael was speaking, but she couldn't hear the words. No, she could listen to them, but her mind was not concentrating. She took a deep breath in and then shook her head. The kids had been moved into care. Lewis was swearing loudly and standing far from the desk, and she was sure that he just needed a few seconds to calm down.

"So, what do we do now?" She finally asked as she rubbed her temples and then looked into the computer since they were doing a video chat.

"I've already filed a few papers to appeal. But it's going to take a bit of time. The best right now is not to lose hope. Just think positive, and as soon as I've heard anything else, I'll be in touch."

"That's not acceptable." Lewis's voice thundered as he leaned closer to the computer. "Michael, those kids can't be lost in the system."

"I understand your frustration Lewis, but this is not a setback. Please believe me. This is just a procedure. They cannot ask the kids if they want to go live with you. You're in another country, so this whole intercountry adoption is hard. Even though you're family, you didn't have much contact with your family, it's all little setbacks, but I can assure you, those kids will end up with you and Seo-Yeon. No one else wants them—"

"Don't say shit like that," Lewis said, furious.

"I know how it sounded, but you know what I mean. You're the only family who wants them, and the government tends to place children with the family when they want the kids."

"How much longer? A single night in those places—"

"Lewis, I promise they're not in a bad environment. I swear. They're all together, all being cared for by people who care and are good."

"We'll wait for your call tomorrow morning then," Seo-Yeon said, knowing that Lewis wasn't likely to give up on thinking that the kids were in some kind of horrible place.

"Maybe we should go to Australia."

"What?" She asked, blinking, and then shook her head. "Honey, we can't just pick up and go. What about the restaurant? The house."

"Then I should go."

"I know you're trying hard to sift through your emotions, but maybe we should sleep on this and then decide," Seo-Yeon said as he took a step back and ran his hands through his hair.

"What if they get stuck in the system forever."

"Michael told you that it's not likely to happen." She reminded him and then took his hand in hers. "I know you're feeling guilty over this," Seo-Yeon said softly as she watched him. "But please, trust Michael at least until tomorrow. We'll have more information, and then we can go from there." She told him.

"I don't know Seo-Yeon—"

"Please, for me?" She asked, pouting.

Lewis groaned as he pulled her into a hug and sighed. "Fine." He said softly, feeling defeated.

***

Seo-Yeon couldn't sleep that night. Whereas Lewis passed out right after dinner, she'd been pacing around the small apartment until she grabbed her phone and climbed the stairs to the rooftop terrace. After sitting down on the big bench used as a table when they barbecued on the deck, she set the bottle of soju down and then dialed Seo-Joon's number.

"Seo-Yeon, are you okay?" He asked, worried as Seo-Yeon took a swig of soju directly from the bottle.

"I'm fine; how are you?"

"Well, I guess since we're lying, I'm fine too."

"Michael called." She explained as she heard Seo-Joon taking a deep breath in.

"What did he say?"

"The system blah blah blah, the kids were removed from the foster parents and taken into care. Which means they're somewhere like a group home or something."

"I bet Lewis is pissed."

"Beyond furious, but we knew it wouldn't be easy." She said having more of the soju.

"Hopefully, the delay is just because they're making sure that you'll be good parents."

"I hope so too." She sighed. "How's Landry?"

"In pain." He said truthfully, taking her by surprise.

"Did you give her the meds?"

"Yes, she wasn't too keen, but I can't see her in pain."

"It's understandable." She frowned, leaning her head against the table while she lay on it.

"I hate seeing her like this." He sighed as she nodded.

"I know."

"So, Michael's take is that you have a chance or not?"

"We do. But it won't be easy."

"We're all rooting for you," Seo-Joon said as Seo-Yeon closed her eyes tightly.

"I think Lewis thought this would be easier because they're his kin." She explained. "But I don't know. I am choosing to trust Michael."

"I think that's a wise decision, and it doesn't matter if it takes a few weeks or months, I believe that he'll come through for you and Lewis."

"Thanks, Seo-Joona."

"Anytime. You're still my favorite sister." He said as a laugh escaped her.

"Dork."

"Come on, I'm not a dork." He said as she opened her eyes and sat up before taking another swig of soju.

"Eomma texted saying you joined some Yoga studio thing?"

"Yeah, well, it's at the hospital. But the patients wanted an early morning activity for those who can still exercise. It was okay."

"It might help you alleviate stress."

"Yeah, maybe."

"Seo-Joon, I know you refused help from Eomma and Appa, so you can take a break, but maybe, you can accept it from Lewis and me?"

"No," Seo-Joon said simply as she nodded. "I want to spend every moment with her. I start my time off in a few days."

"Vacation? Really?" Seo-Yeon blinked.

"I don't want to be at the hospital and get a call from Eomma or Appa."

"I understand that." She said, biting her lip.

"We're going to change the living room into our bedroom. It'll be easier to put all the hospice equipment when the time comes." He added.

"The view is good from there too; she'll enjoy that and be able to see Roxette."

"Yeah," he sighed.

"We can help."

"No, it's okay, we have people from the hospital who'll bring the things. Appa and I have sorted it out. I also went to the cemetery to make sure that everything's ready. Landry was afraid that she would die before she could make arrangements, so we've done that. I think she still felt guilty about her mother being buried straight away without Landry knowing where her mother's body was taken."

"Well, that was never going to happen to her," Seo-Yeon said softly.

"She also keeps making me promise that I'll move on." Seo-Joon's voice choked as Seo-Yeon wished they were still close by so she could go and give him a hug.

"Eventually, you will."

"I don't think so. And I don't think I should be asked to do that anyway."

"Well, I won't ask you," Seo-Yeon told him as she heard footsteps and turned to see Lewis. "I have to go; Lewis just busted me drinking alone."

"Ah, you better go. Thanks for calling."

"Rest." She said as she hung up and then stood up, walking toward him.

"Michael just called."

"Now?" She asked, frowning as he nodded. "What happened?"

"The lawyer who worked for my siblings called Michael and told him that the wills for all of them have me as the possible guardian for the children."

"Possible?"

"If I didn't want the responsibility, they would go in the system."

"So, they're ours?"

"Yes, they're ours," Lewis said as she jumped in his arms, holding on tightly to him.

Chapter twenty-eight

Lewis

Two weeks later

After the mad rush to decorate the house and make sure all the kids had their own bedrooms in the new place, it was time to fly out to Australia. Seo-Yeon's parents promised to keep an eye on the last of the furniture to be delivered. Thus, she and Lewis began their journey into parenthood.

When they arrived in Australia, the terminal was mostly deserted. Lewis walked with Seo-Yeon through customs and then met Michael in the waiting area after picking up their luggage. After ten hours, Lewis just wanted to see the children. After Michael presented the courts with the wills and the petitions, the kids had returned to a foster house, where Michael had been able to see them a few times.

"They're all very excited. I showed them all the pictures that you sent and the pictures of the house and the bedrooms." He said, nodding.

"Good," Lewis frowned. "Did they ask why I didn't come to see them?"

"No, but it seems that Lance knew that you had a falling out with his father, but still, he told me that he'd seen pictures of you at the old house. I guess he meant your father's old farm."

"I guess," Lewis said as they followed him through the parking to the car.

"And we get to see them now?" Seo-Yeon asked as he nodded.

"Yes, we'll go pick them up, and then we just need to go to the court tomorrow, and everything will be over. I also talked to that guy in the Korean embassy. He received all the paperwork, so they should be added to the family register by tomorrow night. He said the passports will be authorized as soon as that's done."

"Good," Seo-Yeon said as she placed her bag in the car's trunk.

"And then we can go back home with them." Lewis grinned at her as she nodded.

"I also have this," Michael said as he opened his briefcase and handed Lewis two files before he opened the car for them to climb in.

"What is this?"

"Psychological evaluations and physicals they are one hundred percent, healthy kids."

"What about the things that happened that night?" Lewis asked, feeling guilty once more.

"Lance seems to have blocked most of it out. The recommendation was to keep him going to therapy once you guys relocate with them."

"He must have been so scared," Seo-Yeon said, looking out the window as the car pulled out of the car park.

"He was, but he put the fear to good use, getting all the kids out. It seems that's why he blocked most of it. He remembers seeing the men with the guns and hearing the gunshots. The doctor didn't think he actually witnessed any violence, but the gunshots might have been enough to scare him." Michael said as they stopped at a traffic light.

"What about the little ones?"

"They're all fine, I mean the babies …" Michael glanced at Lewis then at Seo-Yeon. "How will you deal with five kids under five and a seven-year-old?"

"We found two nannies," Seo-Yeon admitted. "My Eomma and Appa actually did that for us. They thought it would be good to have experienced people help us out rather than us relying on friends or family."

"Well, that's good because it will be a lot of work. I mean a two-month-old baby, a one-year-old, two-year-old, four-year-old twins, and a seven-year-old, it's going to be a lot of work."

"Wait, twins?" Seo-Yeon blinked.

"Yes, didn't I tell you?" Lewis said, glancing at her before he looked ahead when she gave him a stunned look. "Okay, I forgot to tell you."

"Wow," Seo-Yeon said, shaking her head. "Twins."

***

The kids were huddled up together in the living room of the foster parents' home. The babies were in the strollers. As for the rest, they were squeezing together on the sofa. However, once Lance stood up, the others did as well. Michael walked in first before Lewis and Seo-Yeon followed.

"Hi there," Lewis said, trying not to speak too loudly as he looked at Lance and the twins while the little toddler was just toddling around.

"Uncle Lewis?" Lance asked as Lewis noticed that Lance's and the twins' eyes were the same shade of blue as his.

"Yes, and this is Auntie Seo-Yeon." He said as Seo-Yeon stood closer to them and then glanced at the stroller.

"Is it true we'll live with you?" one of the twins asked as Seo-Yeon nodded.

"You're pretty, like a princess." The other twin said as Seo-Yeon squatted so she could look them in the eyes.

"Thank you." She said as she nodded. "What are your names?" She asked as the girl twin smiled.

"I'm Isla, and this is my twin brother, Robert." She said, nodding.

"Oh, I love your name; hello, Robert," Seo-Yeon said, turning to the little boy.

"Are we going with you now?" Lance asked after he pulled at Lewis's jacket's sleeve.

"If you guys are ready, yes, we're going to go, and then we're going to take a plane to South Korea. That's where we're going to live. We've enrolled you in an international school in Seoul, so everything will be in English." He explained as he made sure to look at him in the eye, as Seo-Yeon had told him to do, as she'd read about it in one of the books that Doctor Shim had brought her when they said they were going to adopt a child.

"I'm going to go to school?" Lance asked excitedly as Lewis frowned.

"Have you not been going to school?" He asked as Lance shook his head.

"Dad said it was dangerous, so we were always home in the compound," Lance explained. "But you'll let us go to school with other children?"

"Yes," Lewis said, watching him, wondering if they ever socialized with other kids.

"That's going to be so amazing." He said before he clung to Lewis's neck and hugged him tightly. "Thank you, thank you!"

Lewis, Seo-Yeon, Lance, Isla, Robert, Lilliana, Bella, and Andrew landed in Seoul a few days later. Seo-Yeon's parents, brother, and their friends met them at the airport. The kids were a bit wary of strangers, but when they saw Jun-Myeon, the twins quickly tried saying hello to him, as Seo-Yeon had taught them to say in the airplane.

"Oh, they're adorable." Seo-Yeon's mother said as she looked at them. "Hi, I'm Seo-Yeon's mom." She said to the kids as they all turned to look at her.

"Grandma!" Lance shouted as he gave her a hug before the twins tried to hug her, and Lilliana asked to be picked up.

"And this is Uncle Simon and your cousin Jun-Myeon," Lewis said after giving them a hug, and a high five, which made Jun-Myeon giggle. "And this is Aunt Bom-Hyuk. She's Seo-Yeon's best friend."

"Hello," Isla said as she looked at Bom-Hyuk. "You're pretty too."

"Thank you," Bom-Hyuk told her as she crouched beside her for a moment and then handed the kids a few sweets. "Simon rented a huge van."

"Well, it's a lot of kids." He said defensively.

"It's good, thank you," Lewis said as he looked at the kids while Seo-Yeon pushed the double stroller with Bella and Andrew.

"Oh, the baby's tiny." Her mother said as she nodded.

"He's only three months old," Seo-Yeon said, nodding. "I will be eternally grateful for the nannies, Eomma."

"Has it been hard?" She laughed, watching Seo-Yeon.

"So hard."

"Ah, my poor daughter, welcome to motherhood." She said, patting Seo-Yeon's back before she grinned at Lewis. "It looks good on you."

"What?" Lewis asked, blinking.

"Fatherhood." She said proudly as she looked at him, and Lewis felt slightly self-conscious before thanking her as he held on to the kids, feeling as if he finally knew where he belonged.

Chapter twenty-nine

Seo-Yeon

The day couldn't have started any worse. Seo-Yeon had woken up at three in the morning after going back to sleep at two because the baby kept waking up. Lilliana, their two-year-old, had stumbled into the room. Lewis was already climbing out of bed to put her back in bed when they heard the baby crying again.

"I'll take care of Andrew; Bella is probably up already." She glanced at the clock and then walked out. Lewis picked Lilliana up and took her to the bedroom she was sharing with the twins until they finished the other room she would eventually share with Bella.

"What's wrong?" Lance asked Isla and Robert, quick on his heels.

"I don't know; why don't you all go back to bed?" Seo-Yeon asked as she walked into the nursery and picked Andrew up. "Oh no, where's the thermometer?" She wondered, panicked as Lewis rushed in, still holding on to Liliana before putting her down on the floor and walking in the bathroom with Seo-Yeon.

"It's here." He said, handing it to her before he checked on Bella, who was still sleeping even among the commotion.

"She sleeps really well," Lance told Lewis. "That's what her mom used to like the best; Auntie Belkis always said so."

"Well, I can see why," Lewis told him as Seo-Yeon sighed.

"He has a really high temperature. We should take him to the hospital."

"Sure, let me get the kids ready, and we can go." He said as he ushered them to the bedrooms to get dressed, and Seo-Yeon took care of Andrew and Bella.

She listened carefully as the pediatrician reassured them that everything was fine, but she still had doubts. He smiled too condescendingly, but Seo-Yeon bit back what she wanted to say and let him check Andrew while Lewis waited in the lobby with the kids. She sighed as there was a knock on the door, and her mother walked in.

"Good morning, Doctor Shim." The doctor said as he continued the exam. "Can I help you?"

"You can relax; I'm here as a grandmother." She looked at the baby and then returned her eyes to the doctor. Even though Seo-Yeon's mother had given up practicing medicine, she was still well regarded among her colleagues and the young doctors. She'd worked tirelessly when she'd been seeing patients but had become a full-time administrator a few years ago.

"He's teething. See this little bump." He said, shining a light quickly over the bottom gum of the baby. "That's a tooth. Sometimes it can happen before six months." He said with a nod.

"So that's why he has a fever?" Seo-Yeon asked, confused.

"Yes, he just needs a bit of TLC and something for the fever. I'll send the prescription to the pharmacy; you can pick it up on your way out."

"Thank you." She said, nodding as she started to cry while dressing Andrew once more.

"Thank you, Doctor."

"See you later, Doctor Shim." He said, bowing before he walked out of the room.

"It's fine; you'll have tons of nights like tonight." Her mother said, patting her back as Seo-Yeon nodded.

"It's so scary."

"It is, but you'll get used to this, and then they go off to High School, and your fears start all over again." Her mother said with a sigh. "But the alternative is not caring, and that's just being a bad mother." She added.

"I don't know how I'm going to do this. They were all up. Liliana came in the room; the only one who was still sleeping even in the middle of the chaos was Bella."

"Ah, she'll probably be the troublemaker waiting in the wings, so she can tell on everyone and then get away with murder." Her mother teased her.

"That's not helping."

"I'm super amused; I think it is." She laughed again as they walked out of the room to find Lewis and the kids waiting for them.

"Hi, Grandma." The twins said before Lance could give her a hug.

"Lance, Isla, and Robert came up with a great idea," Lewis said as he took Andrew from her.

"What's that?"

"We'll call you Mom and Dad," Lance announced, still holding on to Seo-Yeon's mother.

"Are you sure?" Seo-Yeon frowned as the kids looked slightly taken aback. "I don't want you to do it if you don't want to."

"We want to, don't you want us to?"

"Of course," Seo-Yeon said, squatting down to his eye level as Lance stared at her.

"You're parents… our parents," Lance told her as she nodded.

"We are indeed." She reassured them. "Can I give you a hug?"

"Yes," Lance said, letting go of Seo-Yeon's mother and hugging her tightly.

"Ah, I'll never get tired of hugs," Seo-Yeon told him before the twins also held on tight to her.

Later that day, when she arrived at work, their manager and staff were all waiting right outside the restaurant. After texting her to let her know that a water line had broken, the place was flooded. Seo-Yeon hadn't expected to find water everywhere. She took a deep breath as she stepped inside and then looked around before waiting for the building manager to finish his chat with the people doing the repairs.

She took a step back and then called Lewis feeling as if nothing else could go wrong. It couldn't. She was ready to go to bed.

"It's going to be fine." He told her and then sighed. "I guess it's not a good time to tell you, Seo-Joon called."

"What's wrong?"

"He asked everyone to go for dinner; I don't think Landry has much longer."

"But we were going to take the kids to meet them this weekend." She said, blinking fast as her eyes welled and tears streamed down her cheeks.

"I know, honey," Lewis said softly when Seo-Yeon didn't say anything else. "Just tell the staff to go home, we'll pay their hours for today, and we'll reopen tomorrow. And if we can't, tell the manager he'll be in charge."

"Do you think… do you think it's really time?" She asked, her voice breaking as she closed her eyes tightly. She'd been so wrapped up in the high she was feeling since bringing the kids to Seoul she'd neglected her brother's pain. She was a terrible sister. And that made her feel like trash.

"I think so, I mean, he texted us, but when I called, it sounded like he's pretty sure that these are the last days. She's deteriorating rapidly, and he's had to increase the painkillers. It seems that she's been sleeping a lot. Rosa arrives in a few hours, so Simon will pick her and Beau up.

"Okay, so I'll pick the kids up."

"No, I'll do that," he told her. "Just go straight home, and we'll all go to Seo-Joon's after I pick you up."

"Okay." She said, nodding slowly before the line went dead, and she stared outside the window. The city of Seoul sprawled in front of her unchanged, even though her heart was breaking. She took a deep breath, deciding that she needed to be strong for her brother, and turned to face the staff. She would relay Lewis's message and then go home. Seo-Yeon forced a smile on her face, walking toward them to do just that.

Chapter thirty
Lewis

The drive from their new house to Seo-Joon's house was barely twenty minutes, but it'd felt like hours. Lewis parked the car right outside the gate, noticing the two other vehicles. Simon and Tae-Hyung's. Doctor Shim's sports' car was parked next to Landry's truck and Seo-Joon's sedan inside the gates. He got out of the car and nodded as Seo-Yeon parked beside him. Lance intuitively knew how bad things were and had helped Lewis get all the kids ready, so they didn't take too much time. He'd also made sure that the kids didn't make too much noise. Something that had stayed with Lewis because Lance had explained that they were really good at pretending not to be there.

He couldn't imagine what sort of things his brothers and sisters made the kids do; did they take them with them on drug runs? Did they know that they were targets of unscrupulous people who didn't care who they killed? After taking a deep breath in, he decided that the kids were safe now, and he didn't need to dwell on those things. He grabbed Bella off her car seat and then undid Andrew's car seat, so he could carry him in the house as Lilliana, Isla and Robert followed Lance.

"They're adorable." Rosa cooed as she and Beau joined them at the gate.

"Thanks," Lewis said proudly as he glanced around, counting the kids to ensure they were all there.

Simon came to the gate to help them and then nodded sadly to Seo-Yeon.

"You guys should go in straight away. I'll take care of the kids." Simon told them as Sara and Tae-Hyung came outside, Jun-Myeon holding on to Sarah's neck as they joined them.

Seo-Yeon held on to Lewis's hand as he nodded. He waited for Beau and Rosa to walk ahead of them and then braced himself for the worst.

The house was so silent it freaked Lewis out. He was used to the hustle and bustle of the city. Living in the countryside had come with its new set of rules and silence. Tons of it. However, where his house was full of laughter and kids running around screaming, Seo-Joon and Landry's house was quite sad. He kicked off his shoes, handing Rosa and Beau the disposable slippers that Seo-Joon had left in a box near the door.

"You guys go ahead." He said to Rosa and Beau as Seo-Yeon was holding on tight to his arm.

"Are you sure?" Rosa asked, looking at Seo-Yeon. It was apparent she didn't want to step on anyone's toes.

"Of course," Seo-Yeon managed to say before she swallowed hard.

"All right." Rosa gave Seo-Yeon a quick hug and then walked to the middle of the hallway, and Seo-Joon met her there.

"Hey, how was your flight?" He asked in a soft tone as Lewis watched them hug, and then he took a step back to let Rosa and Beau walk to the living room.

The whole place had been gutted of the furniture. The hospital bed took up most of the space and the monitors. Lewis nodded when his eyes met Seo-Joon's and then gave him a quick hug before Seo-Yeon held them both in place by hugging them tightly.

"Thanks for coming."

"Of course," Seo-Yeon said, looking at Seo-Joon.

"And picking Rosa and Beau. I wanted to do it—" Seo-Joon told Simon.

"Hey, what are brothers for," Lewis told him with a half-smile before Seo-Joon held on to him once more. "It's going to be fine. We're all here."

"Yeah," he muttered, pulling away. "Where are the kids?"

"They're outside with Tae-Hyung and the others," Simon said. "I'm going to go and check on them." He nodded.

"Have you eaten?" Seo-Yeon asked.

"I don't know, things were terrible this morning, before four, and then… it's been a blur. Mom and Dad got here a few hours ago. She's been cooking so much; I will have to give you guys some food." Seo-Joon said with a dark laugh. "I'm going to have to do some shopping as well. I think she used everything."

"She's probably trying to keep busy," Lewis said while Seo-Joon nodded absently. "I'll go see the kids."

"I'll take you," Lewis said as Seo-Yeon nodded and walked off to the kitchen to give Landry and her friends some privacy.

Lewis found the kids playing in the trampoline Landry and Seo-Joon had bought when they heard that he and Seo-Yeon would take on his nephews and nieces. The kids were already playing with Jun-Myeon, even though they didn't speak the same language. Tae-Hyung and Sarah were translating for the twins as they talked to Jun-Myeon, and Lance checked on Liliana. Anyone driving by would probably think that they were celebrating a kid's birthday instead of being gathered to say goodbye to a sister, a wife, a daughter.

He frowned and then glanced at Seo-Joon before the kids rushed over, led by Lance.

"Hi, are you our uncle Seo?" Isla asked, opening her big eyes as she looked at Seo-Joon.

"I am indeed." He said, squatting down to eye level. "You must be Isla."

"I am, and I'm four."

"Wow, you're so tall." He said with a smile. "You look like your Auntie Landry." He spoke fondly as Isla ran a hand through her long blonde hair.

"Is Auntie Landry sick?" She asked in a whisper as Lewis crouched beside her.

"Isla—"

"Yes, she is," Seo-Joon said, placing a hand on Lewis' shoulder to stop him.

"Is she going to die?" She asked softly as she looked at him.

Seo-Joon nodded, tears pooling in his eyes. "She's going to become an angel soon."

"Our mom is an angel too," Isla said and then covered her mouth. "Our other Mom. She died."

Seo-Joon patted her head and nodded. "But now you have a new dad and mom, and I can tell you, they're going to love you so much, it's going to be hard to breathe sometimes. When that happens, you come to me, okay? I'll get them to back off a bit."

"No, I won't," Isla said with a grin.

"You won't?"

"I like that they love us so much that we can't breathe," Isla told him. "That's why they're Mom and Dad."

"You're so clever," Seo-Joon said, drying the tears from his eyes as Lance offered him a handkerchief with Lewis's initials. "Thank you."

"I'll be your wingman," Lance said as Lewis let out a chuckle, and Seo-Joon couldn't help but laugh as well.

"Wingman, sure." He stood up and then looked behind him as his mother came to greet the kids.

"I'm sorry we tried to explain to them."

"It's all good," Seo-Joon said, looking at him. "It's good, to tell the truth, so they know what's happening." He said, patting his shoulder before he went back up the stairs.

"Are you guys hungry?" Seo-Yeon's mother said as the kids nodded. "Come on, we'll have supper in the dining room." She said, pointing to the garden. "Sarah, bring Jun-Myeon as well, please." She said as she turned to Lewis. "Come on, let's go eat; it will be a long night."

Chapter thirty-one

Seo-Yeon

Even though the house was full of people, it was eerily quiet. There was no wind. No sound from cars driving by outside. It was as if the whole world wanted them to say their goodbyes in peace.

Seo-Yeon stood right outside the door, her eyes on the floorboards, rooted to the spot. When Simon stood beside Seo-Yeon, she took a deep breath and then looked at him.

"I don't know if I can go in there."

"I know," Simon said, patting her shoulder. "It's hard, but she wants to say goodbye."

"I know, but… It feels so unfair."

"I know," Simon replied. "Father Matteo came early to pray. Seo-Joon asked him why this was happening. Father Matteo said something that struck me as the truth. Sometimes God has plans. He lets us derail ourselves to have new experiences; loving passionately and having a family was gifts God gave your brother and Landry. And we should concentrate on that, even if we're in pain over this. She was loved by a family and a husband because her soul is so special."

Seo-Yeon nodded, but the words felt hollow. "Is Lorena here?"

"Yes, she's upstairs resting. The doctor was upset that she's not been resting as much as she should. It's just hard; she wants to do everything for Jun-Myeon even though we have a nanny."

"Well, you don't have long to go now." She said, looking at him. "The baby will be here in two months, right?"

"More or less."

"At least you got a trial run, parenting."

"Jun-Myeon's been great. I just hope that he grows out of being afraid of me." He said sadly.

"He is?"

"Yeah, he witnessed his father abusing his mother. And when she was taken to hospital, He was left alone with her. So, he's afraid of all the monitors."

"Your dad's been keeping him entertained, so he doesn't go in the living room." He said.

"Hey," Beau said, walking closer to them. "I think Rosa wants you to go next."

"Of course," Seo-Yeon said automatically before she walked toward the living room. She stopped right at the entrance before Rosa stood up from the hug she'd given Landry and then beckoned Seo-Yeon to go closer to them.

Landry looked so frail, it scared her to even try to hug her.

"My darling sister," Landry said in a weakened tone as Seo-Yeon gave her a quick hug.

"Hey," Seo-Yeon said as she sat on the edge of the bed and took Landry's hand in hers.

"I saw a photo of the kids; your mom's so happy to have so many grandkids," Landry told her.

"Thanks, they really know how to wrap people around their fingers," Seo-Yeon said. However, she also knew that the kids were really starved for genuine affection and encouragement, and she hoped that she and Lewis could bring out the best in them.

"It's great to see that you and Lewis are already great parents."

"Thank you," Seo-Yeon said, trying hard not to let the tears fall as Landry's eyes closed. She let go of her hand slowly and then watched the monitor before taking a step back.

"She keeps passing out because of the painkillers." Her father said. "I don't think she has long." He whispered so only Seo-Yeon could hear him.

"I'm glad everyone could come over to say goodbye," Seo-Yeon said as her father nodded.

"Come on, let's go back to the kitchen. I promised Jun-Myeon I would get him a fruit," He said as Seo-Joon walked back through the living room and settled beside Landry in the bed.

Later that night, after everyone had gone upstairs to sleep, Seo-Yeon couldn't settle in bed. She walked down the stairs to get water when she stopped dead in her tracks. In the freezing rain, her brother and Landry were outside on the terrace. They were laying down on one of the loungers, his arms cradling her protectively in them, and Roxette was sitting watching them, so still she looked like a statue. Seo-Yeon's first instinct was to yell at him and order him to bring her back inside, but then he heard him.

"Landry, you can go now." He whispered as the drizzle of rain fell over them, and Seo-Yeon stood near the opened sliding door watching them.

"Thank you," Landry muttered back. "Thank you for giving me so much. I'm sorry, I couldn't hold on longer."

"You've been everything to me." Seo-Joon's voice broke as he kissed her forehead.

"This rain," Landry whispered. "it'll take away all the bad memories and leave you with the good ones, right?"

"Yes, I promise."

"Don't be alone."

"I won't be." He choked as he kissed her cheek.

"I'll try to meet you earlier in the next life." She whispered as he showered her with kisses.

Seo-Yeon dried the tears from her eyes, turning on her heels to go to the kitchen when she heard it. She stopped beside him, watching him holding on tight to Landry, as she heard noise from the house's second floor. Roxette howled loudly, but her brother's gut-wrenching scream startled her the most. It sounded more like a wounded animal than a person.

The house came alive almost immediately. The sounds of steps and lights turned on as her parents, and everyone else went down the stairs and then spilled into the living room. Jun-Myeon was picked up by Sarah, and Tae-Hyung followed her, ushering the rest of the kids back upstairs.

Simon and Lewis walked into the terrace, nodding as Seo-Yeon took a step back when Seo-Joon scooped Landry in his arms and then walked back to the living room to lay her down on the bed.

"Simon!' Sarah called from the stairs as everyone turned to look at her. "Sorry," she said, flustered as she cleared her throat. "Lorena's water broke."

"Are you sure?" Simon asked, panicked as Lewis rushed upstairs with him and Seo-Yeon moved to stand next to Seo-Joon.

"They should take Landry's truck," Seo-Joon said as his father came to check on Landry and then made a note in his cellphone.

"I'll drive them." His father said before he looked at Seo-Yeon. "You should call the hospital for Seo-Joon."

"Of course." She said, nodding.

Seo-Joon fell to his knees crying as Seo-Yeon held on to him, trying to comfort him.

"I'll call the hospital and Father Matteo," Lewis said, returning from the second floor as Simon helped Lorena.

"Come on, I'll take you." Doctor Shim said as Simon hesitated.

"There's no time to waste now, Simon." He said in a stern tone as Simon followed them.

Seo-Yeon's mother helped her pull Seo-Joon to his feet, but he wouldn't leave Landry's side.

In silence, the three of them sat for a moment before their mother caressed Landry's face in a motherly way, then kissed her forehead.

"I'm going to miss you, my daughter." She said softly. "You lived a good life, Landry." She added, turning to Seo-Joon, who all but crumbled in her arms crying.

Seo-Joon looked at her and then shook his head. "I can't do this."

"Yes, you can," Seo-Yeon said, holding on to his face to make him look at her. "You're going to be fine. She's no longer in pain. She's no longer in pain, Seo-Joon."
"I know— I'm so selfish; I just wanted a few more days." He said, crumbling against her arms.

Epilogue

Two Years Later

Seo-Joon stepped outside the taxi and then looked up at the group of people standing in the street in front of the large housing building. He put on his sunglasses and then smiled as he noticed Seo-Yeon and Lewis waving at him and all their billion kids copying them. He'd never thought his sister would have taken to being the mom of a huge family so well. She and Lewis were really doing a great job with the children.

"Uncle Seo-Joon!" Jun-Myeon called as he ran toward him, and Seo-Joon picked him up in his arms.

"How's one of my favorite nephews?" He asked him with a smile as Jun-Myeon laughed.

"You always say that because there's so many of us, right? Are we all your favorites?" He asked, laughing as Seo-Joon tickled him. Simon rushed after Haru and picked her up before walking over to where Seo-Joon was with Jun-Myeon. "Hyung, you shouldn't pick him up. He's going to break your back one of these days. He's too big."

"Nah, it's fine. You need to hit the gym harder to pick him up with ease." Seo-Joon teased him as Haru extended her hands for Seo-Joon to pick her up after setting her brother on the ground.

"How was the flight?" Simon asked, ignoring the dig.

"It was good. I see everyone's here already." He said as he could see his parents and Simon's parents talking animatedly near the building entrance, staying in the shade.

"Everyone's here, even a few people we invited but thought wouldn't make it like Onyx and BOS, all my members are here as well. It's really nice. Lorena's so happy. All her Hollywood donors are here too, to ensure a photo opp."

"Even Tae-Hyung?" Seo-Joon asked when he saw Tae-Hyung walking with Sarah.

"Yes," he shook his head disapprovingly, following them with his eyes. "She's going back to Korea in a few months. The new venture he and Sarah started a year ago is going really well. They've also managed to hire a few of the older trainees to earn some money and a few writers." Simon explained. "I still don't like that he's always around her, and I hate to admit it, but his business ideas are excellent." He said, nodding begrudgingly.

Lorena walked to the podium, looking like a million dollars. Seo-Joon was always stunned when he saw her attending glitzy things like this. It seemed in the years that he'd known her that she'd come to be a sister to him. And he was more used to her being a mom than attending red carpets. She'd also become his confidant, someone he could trust not to ask when he would get out there and start dating once more. She understood that he didn't think he could ever get married again.

"Hello, everyone." Lorena began as she greeted the crowd. "I'm so thankful for all of you today. A year ago in South Korea, we opened the pilot program thanks to the government and several trade schools offering training to our residents. Today, I'm proud to announce that The Landry Amos halfway house is opening here in Miami. The Landry Amos Foundation will also offer our residents' trade school training and scholarships for the local Miami Dade Community College. So far, we have ten residents who moved in a month ago. You'll be able to talk to them and ask them about their experiences so far and see where your money has gone." Lorena explained. "So without further ado, I declare The Landry Amos halfway house officially open." She said before unraveling the bow next to her, which was holding a champagne bottle back. The bottle smashed against the side of the building with a loud shattering noise as Lorena took a step back, welcoming the guests through the doors of the building.

"This is so beautiful. Have you been inside?" Seo-Joon's mother asked when she joined him and Simon and the kids.

"Not yet. I'm so glad you and dad could be here."

"Of course, we wouldn't have missed it for the world." His mother replied as she took Jun-Myeon's hand in hers. "Come on, I saw a chocolate fountain inside." She told him as Simon opened and closed his mouth.

"She and my mom keep piling them with sugar and then leaving me to deal with the aftermath," Simon told him as he rushed after them. Seo-Joon couldn't help but laugh at that. His parents had taken to their grandparents' role with ease and were delighted to be able to spoil the kids rotten. He followed the crowd through the doors and then took a glass of champagne from the servers' tray before stopping.

Seo-Joon's heart thumped wildly in his chest. His body remained rooted to the spot while his eyes were glued to the large photo of Landry adorning the wall which separated the lobby from the elevators.

It took a few minutes for him to notice that wasn't the only photo of Landry. There were several others of Landry at work in restaurants, which he guessed Rosa and Beau had provided Lorena with. He recognized the pictures of their wedding, which his father took. Seo-Joon's eyes prickled with tears that he wouldn't allow to fall as he walked around the wall and recognized her voice.

The video of Landry was probably recorded when Seo-Joon had been running errands and Seo-Yeon, and Lorena stayed with her.

"Hello, my name is Landry Amos-Shim. Like many of you, I also ran away from home when I was young and had to live on the streets and do whatever I needed to be safe. When Lorena and Simon talked to me about this building, I couldn't wait to see it. Unfortunately, I will not be able to come to Miami and see their hard work. But I know that providing a safe space for children worldwide and young adults is Lorena and Simon's dream. And I hope that you continue to support them, so they can help even more people. Thank you."

Seo-Yeon placed a hand on his back as Lewis smiled at him.

"Bad surprise?" Lewis asked as Seo-Joon wiped the tears away with his hands.

"Good one." He nodded.

"We also recorded another video where she's welcoming the new residents. She wanted this to be a surprise for you." Seo-Yeon told him.

"It must have been fun for her to do something like this for them."

"It was, and she wanted to do it, so other kids knew that they could succeed even if all the adults around them let them down."

"I just need a bit of time alone." He said, nodding as he excused himself and then walked out of the lobby by the backdoors and to the garden.

Under a sprawling blueish jacaranda tree, Seo-Joon found a photo of Landry and Roxette next to Roxette's ashes. He sighed, taking a sit on the bench and looking at them for a moment before he nodded.

"I tried to keep Roxette with me, but she wanted to go with you so badly," Seo-Joon said, tracing the photo with his finger. "I hope you two are very proud of this place. Simon and Lorena have worked so hard at it." He said as he heard footsteps behind him.

"Are you okay, Hyung?" Simon asked as he patted Seo-Joon's back and then sat beside Seo-Joon. "I told them to warn you."

"I bet Seo-Yeon shut you down." Seo-Joon chuckled softly.

"You know your sister well enough." Lewis chimed in, sitting on the other side of Seo-Joon.

"Landry would have been so proud to have a building like this named after her. I'm sure she would have cried as hard as I'm crying." Seo-Joon said before he laughed.

"Nah, she wouldn't have," Simon said as they laughed. "She would have been telling you off and then asking us to get some Soju or something."

"True." Lewis nodded. "She would have also called your Eomma, and they would both make fun of you."

"Ouch," Seo-Joon said with a half-smile. "I'm really proud of you and Lorena." He said, looking at Simon, who nodded.

"Thanks, Hyung."

"So… I have something to say, but it's a secret," Lewis said, glancing behind them and looking to Seo-Joon and Simon. "And you can't tell a soul because your Eomma and Seo-Yeon will kill me."

"What happened?" Seo-Joon asked, using the handkerchief that Simon had just given him.

"I'm freaking out." Lewis began as he cradled his head between his hands.

"What the heck happened?" Simon asked, worried as Seo-Joon frowned.

"Did you cheat on my sister?" Seo-Joon asked, balling his hand into a fist.

"No, of course not," Lewis said, sitting up straight and looking at them. "Do you think your sister wouldn't have killed me already if I were?" He asked and then took a deep breath in. "Seo-Yeon is pregnant— with twins."

"What?" Simon and Seo-Joon asked in unison.

"Wasn't there a million to one…" Simon started as Lewis gripped his wrist, and Simon groaned in pain. "Hyung, let go."

"I'm never going to be able to sleep again," Lewis said as Seo-Joon gave him the handkerchief.

"It's okay; just bring them over, and I'll take care of them," Seo-Joon said as Lewis's eyes opened wide. "Even at night?"

"Hell no, I sleep at night." He said, standing up before walking to the back door to find his sister.

"Seo-Joon… hey… come on, come on guys, you must babysit at night once… please. Just once a week." He said, following them. Seo-Joon stopped as he crossed the lobby when his phone vibrated. He picked it up and then looked at the text message from the orphanage.

"Did you get the text?" Lorena's voice was nothing but a whisper as she stood right in front of him.

"Right now." He said, looking at her then looking back to his phone. "What does it mean?"

"The process is over; you can go and pick your baby girl now." She said as Seo-Joon shook his head.

"Now?"

"Yes, now."

"What? What does that mean?" Lewis and Simon said together as they stood beside them.

"It means Seo-Joon is officially a dad." Lorena grinned as Seo-Yeon and her parents came closer.

"I need to go now," Seo-Joon said suddenly as he bolted to the door. "Explain the rest to them." He told Lorena before he ran off feeling more alive than he had in the last two years. A daughter was waiting for him, and he had the perfect name for her in Korean and English.

Other Books

Operation Get a Life, Book 1, Bias Wrecker Series
One More Chance, Book two, Seoul Stories Series
Twisted Fate, Book one, Seoul Stories Series
The Disappearance of Camelot, Book one, Stories from the veil
Henry and Gracie

Writing as Marilyn Almodovar

Interred, Book one, Chronicles of the Interred
Fissure, Book two, Chronicles of the Interred
Alternate, Book three, Chronicles of the Interred

Writing as FP Alamo

Corazón, Muleta y Estoque

About the Author

Marilyn Jeulin is the author of "Henry and Gracie" and the YA series "Chronicles of the Interred," she wrote under Marilyn Almodóvar.

Born in the Wild West and raised in a tropical paradise, Marilyn has always thirsted for a good story and adventure. She's a massive fan of Anne Rice, Stephen King, and GRR Martin. And when she's not reading, she's an avid gamer.

She currently lives in Central Florida with the Frenchman and their two children in a house that looks relatively normal until things go bump in the night.

Her next title, "Begin Again, " is the fourth book in the Seoul Stories Series, expected to be published in late 2022.

www.ingramcontent.com/pod-product-compliance
Lightning Source LLC
Chambersburg PA
CBHW052003150726
47999CB00004B/1502